Toytime *Dark* Serie

THE DARK AT BAY CITY

Rando Returns

Corveaux and Luna Millions

Toytime Entertainment 2023

PREFACE

Years ago, on a dark and stormy night on the Oregon Coast, the waves crashed on the beach and the winds howled. The rain pelted the windows and ooded the grounds of the tiny coastal town we called home. Corveaux and I had an idea; an idea that grew from the darkness and into the light.

What if a hero came from the most unlikely of situations to prove it only takes a little hope to change your future?

That idea was The Dark at Bay City.

The Dark at Bay City spawned from a mix of my love of horror and Corveaux's love of storytelling to push the boundaries of expectation and show that even in the darkness, there is always light. Follow along as we tell the story of one small town's dark past and uncover the truth of what's really hiding in the darkness.

-Luna

TABLE OF CONTENTS

Prologue

~ The Darkness Returns ~

Tom Kirkland had lived in Bay City his whole life, a farmer still holding out in the little town from the modernization of the new world happening all along the Northwest Coast.

He watched as the towns around him grew into tourist traps, and if not that, they'd get taken back by the ocean's harsh seasalt air.

Tom's wife had passed several years back, and now it was just him and Bones, his bloodhound. They had a routine.

Every night, old Tom Kirkland would tie up Bones outside to an old tree while he watched his evening programs. About fifteen minutes after doing so, Bones would begin his usual howling; something he would be doing inside had Tom not tied him to the tree.

Bones would sit and howl, only illuminated by the dim yellow light coming through the mesh of Tom's screened porch door.

"Ah, would ya shaddup, Bones!" Kirkland would yell through the mesh, but it would only make Bones howl his long low bellow once again. This would happen every night. It was their routine.

Bones would howl, and Tom would yell, and it was how they both got by, living just outside the city limits, with his old farm butting up to the road where the old dilapidated sign hung.

'Bay City'

An unoriginal name for an unoriginal town. A town full of mostly ordinary people, or so it would seem on the surface, but the truth had been living there with them; just outside of town, in a hole under a stump.

"I said, would you shut the hell up!" Tom Kirkland yelled as he stood to go outside to see what Bones was howling at. He was barking more than his usual melodious horn howls.

The old screen door creaked open as Tom pushed with his free hand, the other clutched at the shotgun he kept beside the entryway.

"If you damn kids are back, by god..." Tom shouted, peering out into the dim woods around his old farmhouse. "Bones!"

Bones whimpered and came running to Tom's side taking in the slack from his leash to get to the porch. He then let out another loud howl.

"Bones! Hush!" Tom shouted down to the loud hound as he walked out into the dimly lit yard. He then began looking out into the trees again, and for a moment, he thought he saw something moving around in the bramble between them.

"Hey!" Tom shouted, raising the scattergun to the dark treeline, "I told you dumb teenagers to stop hanging out in my woods!"

Bones howled again, but this time it was a low and fearful moan of a howl.

"Shut up, Bones!" The old man urged down the dog that was now pulling at his leash to try to get behind the farmer, nudging nervously at his leg.

"Damnit, Bones!" Kirkland kicked angrily at the dog to get him away from his leg, and Bones whimpered, scared of something coming from the dark woods.

Tom peered down the sights of the gun barrel, trying to see anything he could in the darkness.

"Who's there!?" Kirkland shouted out again into the unknown. Bones whimpered again, and continued pulling his line, trying to back away from the woods.

"Some guard dog you are, Bones." The old man said, taking his eyes down from the shotgun to the dog, and in that moment he heard the leaves rustle in the distant trees, and snapped his attention back to woods, now trembling himself.

"I will shoot! You know that!" Kirldand yelled into the wind.

Bones had shrunk into a ball quivering behind the old man, and had his head tucked into his stomach when a sound pulled the dog's head and ears up to attention. In the distance a shadowy figure emerged from the treeline. Too big to be a man, misshapen and malformed.

A weird slimy ooze dripped from the dark figure, and suddenly two glowing eyes emerged from the darkness. Bones yelped, and it spooked Tom so much that his finger slipped and pulled the trigger on the old shotgun, blasting a chunk from the tree Bones was tied to, freeing the leash.

Bones, startled, ran as fast as his old legs would get him away from Tom and the Darkness, dragging his leash and line with him.

Tom Kirkland gulped as the ominous and dark figure began to move towards him, slithering along its slimy way. Tom began to shake as cold sweat began to bead up along his scalp.

"Hey! That was just a warning shot, I won't miss next time!" Tom yelled out to the approaching figure, and it stopped abruptly.

Kirkland let out a small sigh, but then the creature's right arm dropped and hung towards the ground, dripping slime from a large pincer it held instead of a regular hand.

Tom began to back away still holding the shaky gun towards the thing.

"What in the..." Tom fired his second shell from the old double-barreled scattergun, but even with slug rounds he didn't hear any impact. Tom, now terrified, began to turn and started to run back towards the old farmhouse.

The creature's pincer hand opened and it flung it out towards the old farmer, grappling him around the upper torso. Its arm was long and slime ran down, dripping along the ground to its clasping grip.

With a sudden crunch, the creature's long boney claw ripped through Tom Kirkland, bifurcating his body with an eruption of blood as it retracted its hand. The rest of Tom fell to the ground, limp, pouring blood onto the ground in front of his old farmhouse.

Then, satisfied, the creature descended back into the darkness.

The ordinary people of Bay City had forgotten, but in this town there was a legend; a cycle that had continued for longer than time could tell, and for a time, it lived just outside of their city in a hole under a stump.

Now, that cycle had been broken, and the curse it held at bay, the Darkness, was now free. It was free to eat, like it had always wanted to, only it doesn't eat just anything.

It has a very specific hunger.

1

~ On The Scene ~

Emily Sanders wasn't an ordinary detective.

She had been working her way up through the Sheriff's department since she came home from her third tour overseas with the Army Ranger corpse, and found her fiance overdosed on narcotics, days old, in the bedroom closet.

Since then, she had taken every case she could in an effort to advance herself through the ranks faster, in order to become a detective. She picked up extra hours, taking other officer's shifts, just to have access to more casefiles.

Sander's liked a good mystery, too. Her favorite cases always threw her for a loop and that's why she joined the County Sheriff's department instead of the local police; it gave her access to higher profile cases. One's where she could make her mark.

That didn't often bring Emily to Bay City, a small North Coast fishing and farm town tucked between the mountains along the curvy coastal highway.

Town's like it were seldom more than a dark patch on the road to bigger and more bustling beach towns that drew people over the pass from the larger metropolis.

That's where she'd rather be.

Fancying herself as the sunglasses wearing hotshot beach detective like in all the best television dramas. To Emily Sanders, that's where the action was. The crime infested dumpster-lined back alleys littered with sand. Drug addicts trying to pass a fix on a street corner without notice, and informants telling secrets on organized crime attempts that she could foil with little more than good timing.

That wasn't Bay City.

Bay City was a little more than a two mile stretch of curved ocean highway, with a tiny hillside town tucked behind it. On either side of it, was another just as easily forgotten cliffside town, home to vacation rentals and hide-aways for people trying to stay out of the city.

The little strip of industry that ran along the highway was old and run down. It hadn't been remodeled since the last century, and only a few of the buildings still housed businesses.

Emily watched as the local kids walked down the sidewalk snidely eyeing her patrol car as it passed them.

It wasn't often that this town had seen law enforcement that was more than a city cop writing crosswalk violations, and they liked it that way.

The little diner stood out as one of the nicer and newer buildings in the middle of the town intersection, but it too, was still old at this point and the neon on the sign had started to dim in places.

Emily's stomach growled as she made note of the town's only eatery besides what looked like a small ice cream and candy store. The fast food breakfast burrito she had eaten before she left Seaside wasn't settling right, but it wasn't the only thing turning her stomach.

She hadn't asked for this case, it had been assigned to her by her commander due to a lack of expendable staff, which really meant no one else would take it. It wasn't just that the drive down to Bay City was long and to the middle of nowhere, but it was also an odd case.

The local police were declaring it an animal attack, and trying to close the case on those grounds, but the Sheriff's department wanted to confirm before allowing the local police chief to sign off. This put the local police chief in an awkward situation when Detective Sander's arrived from the county office that morning, interrupting his press conference to give him her commander's debrief.

When she arrived on the scene, Emily was met by Officer Jacobs from the local police force, holding a camera strapped around his neck. He walked with her along the police line back to where the remnants of Tom Kirkland's body were still strewn across the grass of his front lawn. Little strips of his overalls and shirt led them to the severed pieces of his arms and torso.

Emily had seen a lot during her time with the military, and even more since she started working at the county, but nothing that compared to the devastating carnage that sat on display in front of the old farmhouse. The cuts left the meat from the body neatly serrated into several clumps and pieces. The blood was thick and coagulated in a pool around the different sections of limbs and parts.

Sheriff Sanders turned, and rushed as she bent over to vomit, trying not to contaminate the crime scene. Suddenly a flash went behind her as Officer Jacobs snapped a crime scene photo of one of the limbs.

"Had to be some sort of animal, no doubt." He said as he snapped another photo, "A bear came down from the woods, or mountain lion, maybe."

"You have got to be kidding me, Jacobs." Sanders stated, wiping her mouth with her sleeve.

"No Ma'am." Officer Jacobs said sternly, "I can't think of anything else that could do this level of damage." He then proceeded to take more pictures with the camera he held, and Emily stopped him, pointing at the device he held.

"Don't you have a guy for that?" She asked, nodding towards the camera. In the city, it would be the forensic analyst's duties to take the crime scene photos. That's what Emily was used to.

"Small town," Jacobs said, smiling while holding up the camera for display, "Some guys are the same guys." he explained, and continued to take pictures of the chalk-outlined body parts.

Emily walked around the mess, trying to make sense of what she was seeing now that her stomach was starting to settle, minus the bad burrito.

"What animal could do this?" She said, thinking out loud at the display. Then, she started to shake her head in disbelief. "Look at his feet." She pointed at the farmer's still planted toes left from where his lower body had just collapsed forward holding them in place.

Officer Jacobs moved in to examine, taking another picture, but Emily just huffed at his apparent joy. She assumed he was just happy to get to play with the police department photography equipment.

"He was just standing there when it happened. He didn't even try to move. What animal does that?" She questioned as she made her examination.

"I don't know, maybe like a big bird talon...swooped down out of the sky." Jacobs joked as he stood back up and rested the camera on his chest. Emily huffed again, not amused by the officer's imagination.

"Not funny...Really, what animal makes giant claw marks like this but doesn't drag or push the body around? It doesn't make any sense. It's more like some kind of machine clamped down on him." Sheriff Sanders postulated while going over the scene.

"Like...a claw machine?" Jacobs joked again, as he made the gesture of a dropping crane claw with his hands.

"Knock it off, Officer." Emily sneered and gave a sly mean eye to the local patrolman who wasn't taking the setting he was in seriously enough for her liking.
Jacob's gulped.

The tone of her voice harked back to her days as a ranger, and in her battalion, there wasn't time for amusement when you had a job to do. Officer Jacob's attitude disturbed her, but she wrote it off as an experience difference between the two of them.

"Sorry, Sheriff." The lower ranked officer shot out with a smirk, "I meant, no offense. I knew Kirkland, it's just strange to see him like this, I guess."

Emily nodded, noting that it was indeed strange to see anyone torn apart the way the old farmer was. She knew it wasn't an animal attack; not from any animal she had ever seen.

Emily stood, investigating the gruesome setting silently as Jacobs watched on. Her training had taught her to be vigilant of anything that would stand out, but everything stood out about this killing. She couldn't help but to shake her head in confusion.

"Does he have any next of kin?" She asked Jacobs without a look in his direction.

"None local. Has a brother down in Arizona; he's already been notified to come identify the body." Jacobs stated nonchalantly as he pulled his camera back up to his eye to continue taking his crime scene photos.

Emily made note of how many different sections the old farmer had been torn into, and how unrecognizable it made him.

"Like anyone would want to see this..." Emily Sanders murmured under her breath still in aghast at the image of it all. "I'll be in town, if you need me."

The Sheriff knew the young local cop wouldn't contact her, but it was a courtesy her position demanded she afford him.

Emily walked back to her cruiser, taking notes in her mind about questions she was going to ask. The fact that the locals were quick to close the case on account of an animal attack was irresponsible to her, when it clearly wasn't, but it wasn't unlike town cops to be less trained and eager to close cases on their own.

Still, she found it suspicious that the police chief would so easily skip over an investigation when the evidence to close the case wasn't supported. This case was now starting to throw her for a loop, and she still felt the sour pit in her stomach as she got back into the driver's seat of her patrol car.

"Something strange is going on in this town." She said aloud as she shifted into gear.

She didn't know why she knew, but she could feel it.

It wasn't just the strange murder, but something smelled in the air that gave her an ominous sensation. It may have been that Emily Sanders hardly came to Bay City or she would realize that the smell had been hanging around this particular town for as long as anyone could remember.

It's just that those who live there seem to have gotten used to it

2

~ A Dick For Mayor ~

Richard Adkins had been mayor of Bay City for going on three terms, and with the next election just around the corner, there was no one running in opposition to him. He was a loud and friendly, obnoxious man who generally got whatever he wanted around town.

He sat in his usual bar seat in the town diner, swilling away coffee faster than little Betty Fowler could keep making fresh pots, and the diner was bustling. Being the only spot in town where anyone could get a hot meal, the diner was patronized by all the locals of Bay City. Mayor Adkins, Dick, as everyone called him, would sit at the end of the bar every morning sucking down the establishment's watery roast as he watched *the news* on the television above.

"Damn migrants! If it wasn't bad enough they ruined their country, now they want to come ruin ours. It's a crisis, I'm telling ya!" Dick burst out as the reporter covered a recent national immigration emergency. It was his usual way of making himself known around town, by calling attention to himself.

The diner door dinged as the Chief of Bay City Police entered the diner and took a seat at the bar next to the disgruntled mayor. Joseph Crocker was only the interim Police Chief, anticipating his full promotion after the previous chief's retirement, but he had already established himself around the city in the few short months he'd held the position.

"There's enough wrong with this country," Crocker said sharply as he took his seat, "Poverty, drugs, crime, taxes...I say fix us first." He continued as he wafted a finger towards the ongoing news report.

"I was just saying that," Dick replied as he patted his new colleague on the back with a smile.

With a nod and wink, Chief Crocker waived over to Betty in an attempt to acquire a cup of coffee of his own. The little waitress beamed a smile back to the man in his upper thirties, and gave a nod to acknowledge him in return. A moment that was broken as Mayor Adkins slurped loudly at his own cup.

"Don't forget me, sweetheart." The mayor said snidely as he held up his empty cup, waving it around in the air, "Damn shame about Kirkland. What do we know?" The mayor questioned, turning his attention back to his fresh police chief.

"I got Jacobs leading the county girl around the old man's farm," Cocker replied hesitantly, "Right now, our best guess is a real bad animal attack, a mauling."

"What kind of animal rips a man apart in his own front yard?" Dick questioned sternly under his breath.

Betty approached holding out the fresh pot of coffee as she walked over to pour the police chief a cup, "Did I just hear the bottom of that cup, mister mayor?" She soothed sweetly, putting on a show as to not let Dick know just how much she despised him for making her put up with his coffee drinking presence every day.

"Thank you, you are a darling, Betty." His mustache twitched from side to side as he smiled oddly at Betty who filled his cup, but she had already turned her attention back to the police chief.

"Cream?" She asked with a raised brow at the officer in uniform.

"No, thank you." Crocker replied sternly with a gulp, "I take it black."

The little waitress giggled automatically as she turned to walk away, taking the pot to another table of guests.

"So, I guess that solves our problem with the other thing." Mayor Adkins quipped as soon as Betty was out of earshot.

"Yeah, bear mauling. Lucky break." The officer replied without looking to the older mayor, instead he just sipped his cup of plain black coffee.

"You don't think little miss sheriff is going to be a problem?" The mayor asked, slurping on his cup as well.

"I don't see why she would be," The chief stated, but before he could finish his sentence, the diner door dinged open, and Sheriff Emily Sanders made her way through the lobby with a huff as she approached the two men sitting at the bar.

"You gotta be kidding me, Crocker." Emily shouted over the big man's shoulder, "You want to call this a bear mauling?" Emily threw a stack of the crime scene photos onto the bar in front of the police chief showing the horrific nature of the attack on farmer Kirkland.

Mayor Adkins caught a glance of one of the photos and began to get choked up at the sight. He stood up abruptly, covering his mouth, and made his way to the back of the diner where the restrooms were.

"Jesus, Sanders." Crocker sighed out, "Those aren't for just anyone to look at! That's confidential police material." He then began to quickly pile the photos back together and flipped them over onto the bar so they couldn't be seen.

"You can't just write this off. An animal doesn't do this!" Emily said exasperated.

"I don't know what else to tell you, Sheriff." Crocker replied without looking up from his coffee, but Emily put her hand on his shoulder, forcefully turning him around in the bar stool, and spilling his coffee onto his shirt.

"You seriously want me to write "bear mauling" on this report? If anyone ever looked into it and saw these pictures, you'd be fools, and worse, I'd look just as stupid." Emily's voice raised loud enough that all of the diner's attention was directed towards her and Crocker. The police chief let out an audible growl at the remark into his coffee.

"Calm down." Crocker spat out as he sat his coffee down and stood from the stool, "Show some discipline. You're in public for Christ's sake. Follow me." The large man then angrily walked out of the diner causing the door to ding once again. Emily scooped up the photos from the bar and dejectedly hurried after him.

Once outside, Emily found Crocker pacing back and forth, stewing in anger in the parking lot next to his patrol car.

"I'm serious, Chief Crocker..." Emily started in, but Crocker growled, interrupting her as he wiped the coffee stain on his shirt, but it didn't go anywhere.

"No, I'm serious goddamnit, Emily." The large man pointed his finger into the chest of the short blonde sheriff, "What do you mean coming into my town, embarrassing me in front of the mayor and these fine people? I don't come down to the surf and shit in your sand, do I? What's the meaning of all this? We're supposed to be cooperating, right?" The spit launched from the cracked lips of the outraged officer as he screamed his interrogation at Emily, but she only stood looking at him unimpressed by his hypocrisy.

"You done, Joey?" Sanders asked with an impatient calmness.

"Damnit, Emily. I'm trying to become Chief permanently here." Crocker added, pleading with Emily to just drop whatever problem she had with the case, and let it close quietly without a big media scene. She knew that's what he meant, even if it wasn't the words he used. "I can't do that with County up my ass every step of the way."

Emily Sanders and Joseph Crocker had known each other growing up. They were both coast kids at one time, each going into law enforcement for different reasons. Joseph had never left the coast, like Emily who had been all over serving in the military, and that gave them different views of the world and how things worked in it. Before then, they were both normal enough kids living life in the Pacific Northwest.

This made Emily feel a little obligated to help Joesph out, feeling a sense of similarity to him, despite their gap in age. Joseph had been a Senior when Emily was still just in grade school, but Emily's older brother, Terry, was friends with him.

Terry had died while on duty when Emily was just a teenager, but she had never forgotten his and Joey's friendship. Still, her sense of duty ate at her.

"You won't stay police chief by kissing the mayor's ass all day. There's some actual police work that needs to be done here. You call this a bear mauling?" Emily holds up the crime scene photos for Crocker to see, "I call it bullshit. That farmer was cut in half, a couple of times, but there wasn't a single bite mark, not a piece of him missing. I know, because you had me over there all morning collecting him up with tweedle dipshit."

"You chose this case, not me, Sheriff." Crocker retorted with a sigh, "I didn't send you anywhere, take it up with your CO if you don't like being here."

The large man turned and began to walk over to his patrol car, "And you owe me a shirt, we have to have these uniforms specially ordered out here in the sticks."

"Hey, wait a second...We're not done here." Emily pursued behind him with the photos still in hand.

Chief Crocker opened the door to his patrol car, and leaned over its edge into Emily's face to stunt her approach, "Sure we are, Emily. Call it a cougar, call it a bear; some animal killed ole farmer Kirkland in his front yard. End of story. You'll get the official report soon enough."

Emily harked out a sarcastic chuckle, "Oh don't think I'm dropping this, *'Chief'*. You can file whatever case report you want, and close it with the city, but I'm not going anywhere. In fact, I'm thinking of requesting to acquisition deputy dipshit as County resources while I'm here working this case."

This made Crocker reply with a laugh of his own, "Jacobs? Take him. He's due for some PTO, and I'm sure he wouldn't mind double-dipping on the County's dime, but Emily, as far as BCPD is concerned, the case is closed."

"We'll see about that." Emily shot back sternly with a grimace as Crocker closed his door separating him from Emily with the glass window.

Crocker gave Emily a dainty wave, wiggling his fingers at her as he roared his patrol car to life, and began to pull away.

"Bullshit." Emily said under her breath to the disappearing patrol car, "Something weird is going on here."

Just then, Mayor Adkins came out of the diner door with another ding of its bell. He was a portly slob of a man in Emily's eyes, but she didn't really know him, she only judged him by his disheveled appearance, uncommon for a man of his position. His shirt tail hung half-tucked out of his slacks, stained and partially buttoned. His hair was combed into a part to try to hide how thin it had become, and his mustache was bushy and unkempt.

He walked up beside Emily who still stood where the Chief's car had pulled away, pulling his pants up around his gut, and trying to tuck his shirt back into them.

"Joseph leave? He only had one cup of coffee." Dick said with honest curiosity, still recovering from his episode in the restroom. "Damn poor thing that happened over at Kirkland's last night." He said, turning his attention directly to the young blonde officer.

"Yeah, sure, Mr. Mayor. A man's been murdered." Emily replied snidely, letting Dick know she wasn't buying his whole innocent politician routine.

"We're calling animal attacks '*murder*' now?" Dick let out with a small laugh that only made Emily's face turn more wry.

"If this was an animal attack, Mr. Adkins, then I'll be the first in line at the beast's feast, but if you ask me, something more sinister is going on here. No bite marks, no tracks. I'm not buying your interim chief's story." Sheriff Sanders cocked a brow at the mayor who had become stoic in his reception.

"I can assure you, Sheriff, if there has been foul play I'll make sure Joseph and the boys get to the bottom of it, but..." The mayor's voice cracked, and his demeanor changed as he recalled the horror of seeing what had happened to farmer Kirkland, "What thing, person or animal, does that to someone? It's unimaginable." He nodded to the photos in Emily's hand.

"Nothing I've ever seen before, Mayor." Emily replied seriously in a way that let Dick know that she was just as horrified by the unknown answer to his query, "But I'm going to find out."

Emily's attention was suddenly steered away as she noticed a kid she recognized walking down the other side of the street.

It was Skylar Bennet, a local preteen that she had run into in the past with his brother Darrin, both new to the coast.

"Excuse me, Mayor." Emily said abruptly as she started to make her way across the highway.

With a gaping mouth, Dick wafted his finger, unable to regain Emily's attention, and soon finding it unnecessary as their conversation was practically over, with neither being able to gain any more information from the other. Dick shrugged his shoulders, turned and made his way back inside the diner for another round of hot coffee.

"Hey! Wait up! Skylar." Emily shouted out across the empty street. She had noticed that he was alone and his pace was hurried. As she got closer, she could see that he was crying and holding his cheek.

Skylar hurried faster as he heard his name called, but he never looked back to see Emily, still in apparent fear from something. She put her hand on his little shoulder to stop him from running from her further, and Skylar finally turned to see her with snot and tears running down his face. Under his hand, was a black eye that he was nursing.

"Jesus kid." Emily said, looking over the boy as he sobbed, "What in the world happened to you?"

Through his tears, Skylar tried to find his voice, "Older kids beat me up on the bus."

"Ms. Applebaum said I can't ride...for a week...because I hit back, and we all got in trouble." He explained as he pulled his hood around to cover his bruised eye. Emily put her finger on his chin and tilted his head up, dropping the hood back down as she inspected the injury to make sure he wouldn't need any kind of medical attention.

"Well, that's a shiner for sure, but it looks like you're going to make it, and..." She pulled her finger away and pointed back across the street to her cruiser sitting in the diner parking lot, "It's your lucky day. Looks like you found a ride. Come on, let's get you home." She smiled as she put her hand back on his shoulder in comfort, directing him to walk with her.

"Hopefully you gave as good as you got. Why are you walking home now anyway, isn't school out at two here in Bay City?" Emily asked with empathic curiosity as they shuffled back to her car.

Skylar just shrugged, "Half day," he said looking at his feet the entire journey.

"Half day?" Emily repeated curiously as they continued.

"What the hell is a half day?" She murmured under her breath as they got into the County cruiser.

3

~ Enter Dave and Marta ~

Marta's hand began to shake as she noticed the uniformed police chief exited the diner. Dave, sitting across from her in the little diner booth next to the window, remained stoic in his seat as he watched Marta fidget nervously. It made him nervous, but not nervous like Marta was.

"I knew we shouldn't have stopped here, David." Marta screeched out in a small raspy whisper.

Dave reached his hand across the table and grabbed Marta's hand in his, clutching it tightly; maybe a little too tightly.

"Calm down, Marta." Dave seethed out through his teeth peering into Marta's aging eyes. "No one is even looking at us. Just stay calm."

Marta huffed out a sigh as her brow twitched. She could hardly calm herself as the adrenaline still coursed through her veins. It probably wasn't a good idea for Dave to suggest that they stop to get coffee before leaving town, but the diner was across from the town's only gas station.

Dave had left the RV parked in their oversized lot after filling the tank, against strong resistance from Marta. Now, she sat nervously looking around the little establishment at all the little people acting so normal; a normal she couldn't feel.

The waitress was making her rounds with the coffee pot, and when she approached Dave and Marta's table, she could see that Marta was unsettled. To the young waitress; however, they merely seemed to be a disgruntled middle-aged couple. Something that wasn't very out of the ordinary in this small cloud-covered slope.

"More coffee, you guys?" The waitress motioned out with the half-full hot coffee pot.

Dave's hand immediately began to raise with objection, "Oh, no thank you. I think we've had just about all we can stand. Any more, and I'm sure I'll float out of this place. Besides, I think the caffeine is giving my wife the jitters." he said quickly with a smile to try to usher the waitress along, but the curious waitress couldn't help but turn to see a now enraged Marta stewing her chair.

Marta's hand snatched up her white porcelain mug and held it up for the young little waitress to fill.

"Are you sure you're ok, ma'am?" The girl asked innocently enough, "I could get the decaf pot." she offered as she thumbed back towards the coffee machine behind the wait station counter.

"Oh, just fill it." Marta demanded with a sneer as she glared over to a disappointed Dave watching the coffee flow back into Marta's mug. Her hand shook as she brought it back down onto the table, spilling a bit as it went. Then, Marta turned back to the waitress who stood smiling as she had finished her task, "That's all, you can go now." Marta blurted out with attitude as she wafted a hand toward the waitress.

The young girl's face turned, and she went along to her next table.

Dave peered back towards Marta after watching the waitress exit earshot, "I said, calm down, Marta. Don't make a scene." He seethed again, this time raising his whispered volume in anger.

Marta's eyebrow shot skyward and curled her face into a look of disgust. She had married Dave twenty-five years ago, and back then, he would have never talked to her so stern like that. He wouldn't have ever gotten her into the situation they were in, but that was Dave then, this was Dave, now.

"You heard that sheriff girl." Marta started in, but quickly quieted her tone back down as she recanted Dave with what she had overheard, "They found a body." She nearly only breathed out.

"Shut up, Marta." Dave demanded, plain and simple, as he darted his eyes around the restaurant to see who might have heard her.

"But, what if..." Marta began to continue, but Dave snapped his attention back to her.

"I said, shut the hell up, Marta!" Dave shouted out, only this time his volume was uncontained, and he accidentally paused the entire room as he drew its attention. The mayor, the waitress, and the other patrons had all turned their eyes toward Dave and Marta's lonely window table.

Marta, without skipping a beat, changed her expression to a semi-believable smile and pulled her hand out from under Dave's, casually patting the back of his as she drew her's away, and waved off the many stares they were receiving.

"My poor husband. Please excuse him. He has tourettes and can't control himself sometimes. I'm sorry y'all...he just needs his medication." Marta said calmly as she reached into her purse and pulled out a small bottle of pills.

She put it on the table in front of Dave. "Go ahead, honey, take your meds."

Dave gulped as he felt the eyes of the entire room piercing through him. He reached down and grabbed the little bottle, snapping the cap loose and pulling out one of the tiny tablets. The room returned back to its louder volume now that the other guests had lost interest in the scene.

Dave swallowed the little pill, washing it down with the last sips of coffee from the bottom of his cup.

"What the hell did you just make me take?" He demanded in a low angered curiosity to Marta.

"I can't tell you, I've shut the hell up, remember?" Marta said coyly as she crossed her arms with a slight grin on her face. Dave sneered. It was little stunts like this one that had defeated him over the years. For Dave and Marta, the fight was all they had left, and it lingered in everything they did together.

The vacation they were on was only an attempt to patch their marriage back up, and Dave knew it. Marta did, too, but she had always held onto the hope that they would eventually figure out their problems and fix their relationship.

"Just tell me." Dave demanded in a huff as he slumped back down into his seat, "am I going to die? Did you just kill me?"

Marta began to laugh, "Oh David, don't be so dramatic." She sang out amidst bursts of laughter before beginning to calm. "If only...It was just your diabetes pill. You needed to take it this morning anyway. Especially after all the syrup you drank with those pancakes. Who needs to calm down, now?"

"Well after last night I'm not sure what to think." Dave groaned out, and Marta's mood changed again.

"What? So, now it's my fault? I wasn't the one driving, but I guess you're going to blame me like you always do!" Marta elevated her voice back up, and Dave's attitude began to change to match hers.

"Shut up, Marta!" Dave wanted to shout, but kept his voice low as he leaned forward and pulled out the wallet from his back pocket. After sifting through its contents, he threw a few dollars and some change down on the table and began to stand. Marta, watching his actions, looked back down to her plate where she still had some food unfinished.

"I wasn't done..." Marta started to chime out, but Dave had already started making his way to the front of the diner and out the door. Marta sighed as she folded her napkin over her silverware on her plate. "Fine. I'm coming. I didn't want to come here, anyway," She said under her breath to herself as she got up and tried to catch up to her angry husband.

Dave and Marta left the diner, and went back across the street to where they had left their RV. A little more dented than it was when they had bought it, but now it was full of gas. Now, they could leave Bay City behind them.

Or, so Marta had hoped.

4

~ Half-Day ~

Skylar sat patiently in the passenger seat of Sheriff Sanders' patrol car, now with his hood pulled back and his face exposed showing his ever-swelling upper cheek. Both him and the sheriff sat in silence as the town passed them by, and they made their way out to the city limits where Skylar lived with his older brother, Darrin. Emily noticed the silence and the melancholy in Skylar's eyes as he watched the trees slowly pass.

"So, where's Darrin hiding these days? He's still taking care of you, isn't he?" Emily questioned to break the silence, but Skylar didn't seem thrilled at the inquiry, curling his lip at its edge in slight disgust at the mention of his brother.

"He's not hiding. He just never goes anywhere." Skylar corrected snidely, but went back to staring out the window and remaining quiet. Emily kept her attention on the road, but couldn't help but feel the awkward mood that the boy was putting off.

Darrin and Skylar had endured a lot over the past couple of years, and she couldn't tell if he was upset from his fight on the bus, or something was going on at home. Darrin was a veteran, like her, only years younger, and had been disabled on active duty. Around that same time, their mom had been in a fatal car accident that had left Skylar in Darrin's custody.

"Well, I know everything has been pretty hard for you two. I'm sure he's doing his best." Emily tried to reassure Skylar and ease the tension in the car. Skylar turned with his brows furrowed and a comically angry look on his face.

"He has a van! He just doesn't want to drive me around, or I wouldn't even have to ride the stupid bus!" Skylar said loudly as he crossed his arms and bounced in the seat next to the sheriff.

"Does he know that you were having problems on the bus?" Emily prodded, hoping to convince Skylar that he might not be seeing the whole picture.

"I tried to tell him..." he whined in reply, "but he never listens. He's always playing that stupid video game with his stupid nerd friends online." Skylar went on to explain. His tone of voice was adolescent in a way that Emily found humorous and she couldn't help but let out a small giggle at his reasoning. That only made Skylar more cross.

"It's not funny!" Skylar huffed out as he flopped out his arms, unfolding them, and dropping them at his sides. "It's all he ever does. He plays that stupid game, and then he eats, then he plays the game some more, then he sleeps. That was what he did yesterday, and the day before that, and last weekend. Everyday, he just does the same thing!"

Emily couldn't help but continue to laugh as Skylar went on, but she eventually had to stop his rant, "O.k., O.k, I'll talk to him." She assured the young boy, and just as soon as she had, they had reached the entrance to the long country driveway that led to the small old house that sat next to a hillside. This was where the two boys lived; just outside the city limits.

Emily put the car in park, and Skylar popped open his door, quickly getting out and making his way to the front door to the old house. Emily proceeded behind him, and followed Skylar inside where Darrin sat on a couch in the middle of the room, staring into a television, and holding a video game controller.

Darrin hadn't noticed them enter due to the headset he wore. Skylar stepped over piles of dirty clothes, empty pizza boxes, and discarded chip bags to get to the other side of the room, and continued into the kitchen setting down his book bag on a table along the way. It crunched a pile of empty wrappers as it landed.

"See what I mean?" Skylar shot out as he passed in front of Darrin, snagging his attention. Darrin turned to see the sheriff standing in his doorway, and dropped his game controller.

"Guys, I have to go AFK, be back in a bit..." Darrin said into his headset microphone as he stared at Emily, and then he took it off and placed it on the table in front of him, "Hello, Sheriff Sanders, what did Skylar do to make you have to come here?" Darrin asked as he propped himself up to stand on his uncovered prosthetic leg.

"I just saw him walking down the road, actually, and figured I'd give him a ride home." Emily looked around at the boy's living conditions and found everything to be untidy, but nothing out of the ordinary for two teenage kids living by themselves, " Skylar needs to tell you about his fight on the bus, and his black eye."

Darrin looked over to Skylar who was standing in the threshold of the kitchen listening to their conversation, but trying not to look like it.
"Yeah, it's kind of hard to miss it. He was telling me some kid on the bus was making fun of him and said some joke about our mom." Darrin gave Skylar a hard stare.

"We talked about it, and I had kinda hoped it would work itself out." Darrin explained calmly, and it made Emily feel more comfortable about the whole situation.

She leaned against the wall, momentarily, making herself more at home.

"I see." Emily sighed, "I guess Skylar thought that you hadn't heard him, and he just wanted me to talk to you about it. How's everything here holding up?" Emily nosed to a stack of empty pizza boxes that looked like they might fall over and off the end table that stood between her and him.

Darrin grinned childishly, and grabbed up the boxes, tossing them into the kitchen past Skylar. "Everything is just fine here, Sheriff." Darrin limped over to the coffee table and picked up a handful of empty bags, "Military still pays for everything, and as you can see, we're not starving or anything." Darrin tossed the bags into the kitchen, and continued to tidy around the large room, hobbling on his fake leg.

"You don't have to clean for me." Emily said plainly in unease of watching the disabled man move about, "I just wanted to see Skylar home and safe. I'll just be on my way, and let you two get back to eating the ass-end out of a convenience store." She smiled and turned, heading back towards her patrol cruiser. Darrin managed his way to the door, and locked it as the sheriff left sight.

"Your new best friend, I take it?" Darrin shot out snidely to Skylar as he turned and hobbled back to the couch, picking up his controller from where he had dropped it before.

"Emily is a nice person. You wouldn't know what that's like, because you're a butt lick!" Skylar snarled out in retort to his brother's attitude. Then, Skylar went back into the kitchen to prepare his afternoon snack; a giant bowl of cheese puffs and a two liter bottle of soda. It wasn't an unusual meal, not in their house, not for Skylar.

Darrin put his headset back on and rejoined his friends waiting for him online on the video game. He adjusted the microphone into place, and positioned himself into a comfortable spot on his couch. A couch that he sat on all of most days, and slept on most of all nights. The house might have been his, but the couch was where he lived.

"Alright guys, I'm back!" Darrin sang excitedly into his microphone.

"Wait? What?" Darrin's tone changed, "What does he mean, he wants us all to meet up? I don't ever do meet-ups! I just play this game and move his credits around, I don't leave the house!" Darrin became incensed.

Skylar peered around the kitchen doorway to hear what Darrin was yelling about, "What do you mean, he's not going to pay? He has to pay!"

Darrin's thumbs flicked the joysticks around, moving the little digital man on the screen, and silence ensued. Skylar returned to his over--sized snack and lost his attention on Darrin, and gave it to a screen of his own; a small phone screen he used to watch his videos.

"What time tomorrow?" Darrin asked the video game people. His mood was less intense, more somber now. "Fine. If we have to, we have to. I'll pick you up in the van, in the morning."

Darrin kepting flicking the little sticks and pressing buttons, and Skylar snacked, watching his screen. This was their routine. It was an average life in Bay City.

For now.

5

~ The Only Laundromat in Town ~

Before they could leave town, Marta insisted that Dave stopped by the local laundromat and that they washed their clothes. The clothes from the night before. Dave had forgotten that they were still in the laundromat's dryer after the scene that Marta had made him endure at the diner, and they had to turn around and go back to Bay City, once again.

Much to the townsfolk's disdain, Dave pulled the long camper through the narrow boardwalk lane, and parked alongside the front of the laundromat. He huffed as he slammed the door on the RV, getting out.

"Make sure they're done!" Marta yelled through the open window, "You know what I mean." She added in an odd tone. Dave just nodded with a disgruntled look back to Marta.

When Dave entered the small room-sized laundromat, he noticed one of the local teens sitting on top of the dryer that he had used to dry their clothes. The dryer's time had expired, and Jay had felt it would be a warm spot for his postier while he loitered with his friend Duck.

Of course, Duck wasn't his real name, but most of the older kids in town went by silly nicknames to avoid getting a reputation on paper. It never really worked, though, and most of them started being watched by the police, or ended up having to leave Bay City to find bigger and brighter futures before washing out to sea on a crab boat.

Dave walked up to the clothes drying machine, and looked up at Jay, "You mind, kid?" Dave shot out, pointing at his clothes still in the dryer.

Jay slowly turned his head towards Dave with wide eyes, feeling interrupted. Then, he suddenly switched his expression to a sarcastic smile, "Right on, relic." He smirked out with a grin, "It's your spin."

Then, Jay popped off the machine near-acrobatically landing on the floor of the laundromat, and took a bow before standing next to Duck.

Duck clapped sarcastically in reply.

"Are you done?" Dave nosed the question towards the teens, and Jay only sneered back, before Dave popped open the machine and pulled out a shirt that was still damp and had a big red stain on it. He crumpled it in his hands as they shook and wrenched the shirt in anger. Then, Dave turned towards the large glass front window and showed the shirt to Marta.

She squinted through the RV window to see an upset Dave displaying a shirt no better than it was the night before.

"You'll have to run it again!" She yelled through the two windows, "With bleach this time!" she continued to hark.

"Holy shit! Who'd you kill, old man?" Jay laughed out as he nudged an elbow into Duck's side as if to transmit the crude humor physically. Duck indeed followed suit with an odd chuckle of his own.

Dave gave the two teens an annoyed look before starting to pull out the clothes from the dryer and beginning to load them back into the only working washing machine.

As he did, Duck couldn't help but notice that the few shirts and pants were covered in stains. Once Dave finished reloading the machine, he reached for his wallet and began walking to the change vending machine; however, Dave had given all of his small bills to the table at the diner.

"Damnit. I can't make change." Dave muttered out aloud, and Jay perked up from his lean against the wall. "Hey, Marta!" Dave yelled out through the door of the small glassed room, "Do you have any quarters?"

"You won't even let me have the bank card anymore!" Marta shouted back with a wry glance, and Dave slumped his shoulders in defeat.

"I can make some change for ya, pops." Jay said low as he approached Dave closer, tapping his chest pocket and indicating that he had some product for sale. "You know, if you want to have a little fun." Jay smiled. Dave's brows narrowed, and Jay took an alarmed step backwards.

"I think I'll just go next door." Dave growled out in a scary low voice of his own.

"Right on, old man. Right on." Jay grinned again, this time turning to see Marta leaning over to watch through the motorhome window. Jay winked at Marta and gave her a nod, "Well, you'll know where to find me, when you change your mind."

Marta recoiled back into her seat feeling visually violated by the awkwardly lustful teenager, and Dave shouldered his way past Jay and Duck to get through the laundromat doorway and back out to the street.

Next door was a small convenience store.

~ The Store Next Door ~

Joe had immigrated from China when he was a young man, and he had come to Bay City on his journey through America. A journey that ended in Bay City. Once Joe had found himself sitting behind the counter at his store, the years seemed to just pass Joe by as he sat and read the daily papers, over and over, each day.

Joe was an old man, now, and all he wanted was to enjoy the time he spent sitting in his chair, ringing up customers on his old analog cash register, and reading and watching the news.

It had saddened Joe that the city had become a mere tourist stop, and it brought in all kinds of people. The extras and the local teens had kept Joe's faith in people low, and he didn't seem to mind letting the irregulars know it. So, Joe sat, and time passed; customers came and went as fast as the tides.

"Two forty-five." Joe chimed out with a thick chinese-american accent that he had never managed to tame. "Two one dollars, one quarter, two dime!" He continued with his unnecessary explanation to the large sleeveless lumberjack of a man holding a small bottle of orange juice across the counter.

Before Rando could pay for his juice, Dave came in with a small bell chime from the store's entrance holding a twenty dollar bill.

"Hi there." Dave said to the two onlooking men, "I just need some change for the laundry machines." He explained as he approached the counter and Joe, stepping in front of the ominously sized man with darkened eyes. Rando didn't seem to notice the discourtesy, but Joe always noticed. Joe's finger immediately, as if trained, shot towards a small little hand-written cardboard sign that perched atop the old register's digital display.

It read, *"No Change for Laundry!"*

Rando made a second attempt to hand Joe the few bills he held, but Dave interrupted them once again, "Come on, it's not like I need twenty dollars worth of quarters. I just need to do one load. Can't you just open the little drawer, and give me a few bills; maybe a ten, some ones, and then like a handful of quarters." Dave illustrated by motioning his hands as if to demonstrate the simple process it would take for Joe to accommodate him.

Rando's third attempt sent his bulky arm around Dave, placing three dollars on the counter in front of Joe. Joe nodded back to Rando as he took the money, placed the change into Rando's giant blistered and waiting palm, and shut the drawer closed again.

Rando grunted his usual grunt as he passed around Dave and out of the store, saying nothing else but a grunt.

"See! Right then! You could have kept the register open and have given me the change I need!" Dave shouted at Joe, who said nothing in reply, and instead just stared his small squinty stare back at Dave.

Dave became irate at that moment, losing himself to the darkness that had stalked this town. "Don't you understand! You take my bigger money, and you make it smaller money! You stupid immigrant!" Dave shouted at Joe; a man he had never known.

Joe's mouth curled at the edges unimpressed with Dave's slur, and he again pointed to the little sign that sat on the register.

"No Change for Laundry." He said plainly in his thick accent. Dave's hands shot up wildly beside him and then back down just as quick. Joe shrugged his shoulders with no further explanation to Dave for the lack of accommodation.

"Yeah, thanks..." Dave murmured as he turned to walk back outside. Joe propped an elbow down on his counter and rested his chin in the cup of his hand as he watched Dave exit his store. "Stupid Jap..." He could hear Dave mumble as the door closed behind him, and it was enough insult for Joe to pop back up in astonishment.

"Stupid fat American, why not eat another cheeseburger, eh." Joe said under his breath, wafting his hand around in the air, "I'm Chinese, not Jap. Stupid." His thick old accent sped out the words, and Joe turned his gaze in disgust away from the door.

Angrily, Joe threw two corn dogs into the fryer.

People came for the corn dogs. They came for the cheap drinks and ocean view, and they came to try to get change for the laundry, but really; they came for Joe. Joe had always been there, and as far as most people were concerned, even Joe himself, he would always be there.

Joe had become a part of the town; for better or worse.

~ Here Comes Wendy Pottercorn ~

Marta watched through the rear-view mirror as Dave made his way back to the motorhome.

"Did you get quarters?" Marta yelled back to Dave as he got closer. Dave's fist clenched around the twenty dollar bill, and his teeth dug down into his lower lip as he tried not to swear. Marta could tell her answer by looking at him, and pulled herself back into the seat again.

"Damnit!" Dave yelled out, turning to re-enter the little inconvenient store.

While Marta sat waiting for Dave, she noticed a woman walking towards her. She was a tall slender woman wearing big sunglasses and had herself made up like an old-fashioned magazine model from a long-forgotten era of old fashion magazines. Marta couldn't help but feel a bit of dread wash over her as the woman advanced, and tapped her white-gloved knuckles on the side of the camper.

"Hello there! I'm Wendy, are you new to town?" Wendy asked as she spread out a smile full of pearly white teeth. Marta couldn't find the words to answer back, and instead stared blankly back at Wendy.

"Oh, come on, now. Don't be shy. It's a small town, and we're bound to meet sooner or later. So, I figured why not sooner, and I just came over to introduce myself and welcome you to town." Wendy went on to explain, and Marta began to relax.

"Oh, that's ok." Marta said, wafting her hand through the window as if to politely excuse the strange woman . "We were just staying down at the R.V. Park, but we're leaving now."

"Crazy time to be passing through here." Wendy warned, and Marta's eyes widened in curiosity at the statement.

"Why do you say that?" Marta leaned out to get in better earshot of Wendy. She didn't know what kind of local gossip she was about to hear, but she hoped it wasn't anything she already knew about.

"Didn't you see the Sheriff? All the cops at the diner this morning?" Wendy's lip turned out at the top as she interrogated Marta, giving away the origin of her south sounding draw. "They're saying something happened to old farmer Kirkland, just outside of town; some kind of attack or something."

"That's horrible." Marta said with an almost artificial gasp.

"It's really weird. We don't get too many of those here." Wendy noted as something drew her attention down the street. She shielded her eyes to get a better view. "That's odd. There's his dog, right there." Wendy pointed towards a speck on the edge of the hazy heat blurred horizon that slowly became Bones as it came into view; Tom Kirkland's dog.

Bones ran up to Rando as he was entering the shop on the other side of the street. Wendy watched as the big man bent down to pet the little lost dog.

"Mmm. That boy." She said, and then suddenly snapped her attention back to Marta, "Poor little thing. It must have gotten away somehow, and now he's lost." Wendy said, making a pouty lipped expression, "I better go help. It was nice to meet you!"

Wendy began to run toward the dog, clicking her heels as she crossed the pavement, "Bones! Here boy!" Wendy sang out.

Marta sighed in relief that the interaction was over, and just long enough. Through the mirror she watched as Dave exited the store once again, this time, holding a dripping hardly-covered cheeseburger in one hand.

"A goddamn cheeseburger, Dave!" Marta yelled back out through the window, and Dave's overly excited head snapped towards her flinging ketchup from his lips as the jostling momentum stopped.

"I had..." Dave chewed a wad of meat and greasy cheese, trying to swallow it down, "...to get change." he gulped.

"We just ate!" Marta exclaimed, noting their extremely previous meal.

"When I'm nervous, I get hungry." Dave chomped down on his burger, watching Wendy across the street, bending over to pick up Bones, and admiring what he saw, "You know that." Cheese and mayonnaise stuck to the sides of his lips that was only pulled back into his maw by the spinning lashes of his searching tongue.

"What did she want?" Dave asked, not taking his attention away from the skinny Wendy on the other side of the road.

"It wasn't anything to do with you, moron!" Marta pierced out through Dave's lost attention, "Go, finish washing the clothes." She demanded, and Dave shrugged as he absorbed another mouth's-worth of heart-clogging meat mass; turning back to the laundromat.

At this point, Marta wasn't able to take much more. She wanted to leave, but she felt trapped. She was done with Bay City, but it was becoming clear to Marta that Bay City wasn't done with her or Dave, and the day drew on.

~ A Human Stain ~

Marta got out of the camper and followed Dave back inside the laundromat where he was met by Jay and Duck on their way out. Jay moved to block Dave's entrance, forcing Dave to bump into him on his way in. Jay turned and rammed his chest into Dave and bounced off, only to continue his performance by pounding on his chest like an ape, wildly taunting Dave.

Dave began to ball his fist and draw it back as if he were going to punch Jay, but Marta grabbed Dave's wrist and stopped him. Dave looked back disappointed at Marta, but Jay and Duck only began to laugh and point as they seemed to dance out through the doorway.

"What were you just thinking?" Marta scolded, and Dave continued to the washing machine to add the quarters his cheeseburger purchase had awarded him.

"You have to stand up to little punks like that." Dave explained, pulling out one of the shirts, "Nobody else has taught them any manners. Sooner or later, the world is going to. Today, I just happened to be the world...or would have been had you not stopped me." Dave said with some hint of resentment as he stared out through the glass where Jay and Duck still stood laughing.

"Oh sure, you're the world, David." Marta chuckled out sarcastically, then she extended her palm to receive something unknown from him, "I need a dollar for the changer." She declared as she awaited her money. Dave, still dumping quarters into the washing machine, looked up at Marta, whose hand nearly jabbed him in the face as he turned, and he huffed in disappointment.

Dave pulled out his wallet and handed it to Marta, whole. She grinned and pranced over to the bill changer. "Besides, you're a man. You're supposed to be more mature than some little surfer brat." Dave huffed again as he put in the last quarter, turning on the machine and filling the room with a small rumble of a noise.

"Just shut up, Marta." He muttered under his breath as he watched the two hooligans leaning against the glass outside. Jay and Duck were looking back at Dave, making faces and rubbing their various appendages against the glass as they laughed.

Dave thought about the night before. He thought about the clothes in the wash, and why they were in the wash. Marta seemed to walk around without a care; maybe nervous and a little scared, but she wasn't experiencing the same soul crushing paranoia that Dave felt, after all, he was the one driving.

The two thugs giving him a hard time now, probably wouldn't, if they only knew.

Dave had blood on his hands.

6

~ In the Pocket ~

Jay bounced back and forth against the glass of the laundromat storefront until abruptly coming to a stop and shooting himself forward onto the sidewalk where he began to pace. Duck watched on with a strange excitement, grinning a strange grin, when suddenly, Jay stopped pacing and pointed his top two fingers at Duck.

"Old shits." he said to Duck, stern and direct. Duck only nodded, grinning his same weird grin in agreement with whatever he thought Jay meant. Then, their eyes were drawn away by the passing patrol cruiser of the local town chief.

Jay shot his hands into the air as he spun, "Old shits!" he yelled out into the sky. Then, he turned back to Duck, staring strangely intent at him. "It's old shits." Jay stated once more, and Duck continued to nod.

"It's been a month since that old shit shot Merph in the woods!" Jay began loudly, "I didn't see all the PD rolling around for that." He continued as he pointed down the street to the chief's car.

"Just because his mom was on the glass. Shit. Now, no one has seen Tux since last night." Jay poked Duck in the chest, "You heard from him?"

Smiling, Duck shook his head, "Nah, man. Nothing."

Jay began to pace again, "His mom tried to file a report this morning, but these old shits told her that it hadn't been long enough, and that she had to wait! They aren't doing a damn thing!" Jay shouted out down the street. "Oh, but one old farmer dropped dead on his front porch, and now they got the whole county down here. It's so stupid!.. Let's walk." Jay twisted his feet and turned in the direction he wanted Duck to follow, and they began to walk down the street and away from the laundromat.

"All I'm saying is, something isn't right." Jay attempted at a conclusion as they made their way down the sidewalk. "The whole time we're growing up we're told to respect our elders, say our *yes ma'ams* and *no sirs*, and for what?" So they can just abandon us when one of theirs needs to go first? It ain't right!" Jay lectured and Duck followed along.

They turned a corner that led them down an old alleyway. Duck looked up at the fire escapes and hanging wires. The store lights flickered as they walked; the lights that still worked at least, and Jay kept his gripe going as he kicked rocks along the brick corridor.

"I mean, what about Merph now that the old farmer bit it? Will he ever get justice? I don't think so. They'll just sweep it all up, nice and neat. Like they do." Jay snarled and kicked one of the rocks a little harder than he had been doing it, and it shot across the alley floor into an old metal trash can. The ringing sound it made scared Duck so bad he jumped back. Jay could tell Duck was a little jumpy, but they were almost to the other side of the alley.

"Shit!" Duck shouted out, "I could have pissed myself." He huffed, and Jay started to laugh at his nervous attitude.

"Come on, we're turning just up here." Jay managed out between little cackles as he turned to exit the alley. Before he could complete his twist, Jay was halted by the front of a police car, almost hitting him, if Jay had not paused a step. Suddenly, red and blue lights flashed on the patrol car and spun their colors around the alley's exit. Jay slapped his hands across the hood of the vehicle in anger.

"Hey, what the hell! You could have run me over." He yelled through the windshield at the unknown patrolman.

The door to the cruiser opened and out stepped Officer Jacobs. Jacobs walked slowly around to Jay, who was backing away from the officer. The much taller policeman pushed his fingers into Jay's chest, forcing him against the alley wall.

"What are you goons out selling today? Come on, let me see it." The officer commanded menacingly, but Jay just turned his face away from the ever-approaching Jacobs. His hand searched around in Jay's clothes until finally finding a pill bottle in his inside chest pocket. "There we go. Jackpot, eh Jeffy?" Officer Jacobs grinned an evil grin as he clutched the teen.

"Hey man, not cool. I need those for my...Dyslexia." Jay tried to convince the young officer, "I have to take those or I can't read nothing." Jay couldn't help but giggle at his own absurdity, and the officer didn't seem as amused. Instead Jacobs turned the bottle and read the pharmacy label out loud to the punk teenager.

"Percocet. Hmph..." Officer Jacobs narrowed one brow, and cocked the other, "For Jeanie May Turnhil, date of birth, May twenty-two nineteen forty-seven." Jacobs evened his brows angrily.

"So what then? You had one of those backwards aging sex changings? It must have hurt." Jacobs laughed awkwardly at his own joke, and spun the bottle in his hand, sliding it into his pants pocket.

Then, he started to walk back to his patrol car.

Jay and Duck looked at each other, both angered by the event.

"Prick." Jay muttered out under his breath, but not out of earshot of the easily antagonized patrolman. Jacobs stopped his stride, and pulled the pill bottle back out of his pocket, bouncing it in his hand before tossing it into the passenger seat of his car. The officer turned and made his way back to Jay with an increased speed in his step that he didn't have before.

Jacobs grabbed Jay by the wrist, and turned him, smacking his face against the alley wall before kicking his legs apart.

"You think I'm what? I'm a prick? Is that what you said?" Jacobs leaned in close, talking loudly into Jay's ear. Duck started to advance, but Jacobs shot a quick angered glance that held him at bay.

"I could take your little punk ass down to the station, waste my time filling out paperwork, and let you sit in a holding cell until your rich prick parents come and buy your ass out. I was just saving us both some time." Jacobs growled out as he pushed Jay's face into the brick, forcing him to spit out a lip full of blood.

"You corrupt mother..." Jay started to slur, but Jacobs pushed his face against the bricks again to shut him up.

"You can't do that!" Duck called out in cracked intensity, and Jacobs turned to renew his dominating gaze at Duck, only this time, Jay had the opportunity to land a blow on the policeman, turning and punching him in the ribs.

Jay didn't stop with getting a shot in on Jacobs, instead he continued to pummel on the officer as he recoiled. Duck joined in and began kicking at Jacobs' legs.

One of Jay's blows connected with Officer Jacobs and sent him staggering backwards onto the hood of the patrol car, giving Jacobs the distance he needed to pull his sidearm.

He fired a round in the alley to halt the teenagers assault. The shot rang out loud and both Duck and Jay clasped at their ears.

"Get back! You little shits!" Jacobs howled, bleeding from the edge of his lip and forehead as he pointed the gun down the alleyway at the two teens. Duck's arms shot skyward, and Jay began a series of motions that he couldn't control as he tried to run.

"Holy crap!" Duck shouted, "Don't shoot us, man! My mom would be so mad." He tried to explain as tears began to form under his eyelids. Jay began to run back down the alley, knocking over piles of trash along the way.

"Go, follow your friend!" Jacobs urged as he motioned down the alley with the pistol. Then, a small electronic noise emitted from the patrol car's police radio, and a muffled voice came through. The sound scared Duck enough to send him running behind Jay down the alley.

"*All units respond. Intersection of Miami and Highway one-o-one. All units respond. Body of a teenage male has been found at the roadside. Possibly deceased.*" The dispatcher alerted, and Jacobs backed up to the patrol car still holding his weapon ready. He wiped his lip with his free hand and then used it to grab his radio.

"Unit six en route..." Jacobs replied looking at the blood on the back of his hand, "...E.t.a five minutes." He clicked the button to end his transmission and sat slumping into his cruiser, holstering his pistol, and enclosing himself as he shut the door.

The blue and red lights danced wildly around and around. He looked down at the little bottle of painkillers he managed to acquire from the local teens, and smiled as he grabbed it.

The patrol car roared to life, and Jacobs turned on the siren as he sped down the highway to the call just minutes away, not giving another thought to the event he had just had with Duck and Jay.

Officer Jacobs was back on duty.

7

~ Roadkill ~

Officer Marlon was standing over the body taking notes, when Officer Jacobs arrived. Marlon had worked for the Bay City police department longer than Jacobs, and didn't care for Jacobs' cavalier attitude at crime scenes, but it was a small town and they often worked together.

"Another bear mauling?" Jacobs mused as he approached, tucking in his uniform before seeing the horribly mutilated body of the teenage boy on the ground in front of Marlon. It had been torn apart, but not in the same way that Tom Kirkland had been. This was done by a different kind of beast.

"Jesus H...holy shit!" Jacobs called out in astonishment as he observed the scene.

"I doubt it," Marlon turned an eye towards his bewildered fellow officer. "It was probably more like a Fleetwood, or an Itasca." Marlon continued, but Jacobs just shot back a disbelieving expression in return.

"What?" Jacobs questioned building up a sarcastic tone, "How can you tell?" The young officer walked around looking at the gory display of parts, "Is that fancy detective college training kicking in? Are you already putting all the pieces together, brainiac? You're like one of those Eight O'clock television shows where the detective has superpowers of observation."

Marlon's eyebrow pulled upward as he waited for Jacobs' diatribe to end. Then, he walked across the body and into the taller grass that led to a curve just down the roadside. Blood was splattered around the ground and a backpack sat alone in the grass. A few more feet revealed a broken and bent bicycle bedding down the glass near the shoulder of the highway.

Jacobs followed as Marlon showed him what he had already found.

"Actually, I just found this blood a little ways from the body. Then, I saw that backpack, so I kept walking. That's when I came across the bicycle. I thought back to the kid, all bashed to shit like that..." Marlon exaggerated as he explained, "You see, I began to piece together the events in my superbrain and judging from the damage, I was thinking it had to be something big like a truck." Marlon's lip curled at the edge in disappointment. He never had found Jacobs to be the brightest on the force, and he wasn't afraid to let that come out in how he talked to him.

"Looks like he got clipped while riding his bike."
Jacobs replied in summary of Officer Marlon's explanation.
He walked along the path Marlon had made to see the bike
laying in the grass.

"No shit. I just said that." Marlon stated exasperated.
"Jacobs you're as sharp as a butter knife." Jacobs smiled,
misunderstanding the slight.

"Thank you." Jacobs said with a goofily satisfied grin.
"Did you find any identification on him?" He asked, a little
sure of himself, and hoped that he had somehow reminded
Marlon how to be a better officer by his excellent example.

"I think this one's a little young for a driver's license,
mister detective. The bike didn't give that away?" Marlon
quipped, and Jacobs rubbed the back of his head. "They'll
likely try to get prints from the handlebars, but even that's a
longshot. He'd already have to be in the database." Marlon
went on to explain, and Jacobs nodded understandingly.

"Poor kid, never even saw it coming." Jacobs noted
casually.

"Oh, he saw it. Most likely, it hit him dead on coming from the other side of the highway." Marlon pointed to some tire marks that trailed along the road indicating that someone had tried to maneuver a large vehicle. "Smack! Right in the forehead." Marlon clapped his hands together to give noise to his remark.

"Damn. Yeah, no wonder he's so messed up." Jacobs stated as he walked back to his patrol car. "I'll go file the report, and leave a spot open for your notes, but just be brief, will ya? Your girlfriend is in town, and we don't need to give her any reasons to stick around. She's already looking into the Tom Kirkland case."

"Emily's here?" Marlon perked up. He and Emily Sanders had a long history that went back to when he first moved to the coast; however, he hadn't seen her in some years. This made Marlon both excited and nervous to know they may cross paths again.

Jacobs turned back as he opened the door to his cruiser. "Yeah, but we don't need her looking into anything else, this or the Murphy case. She's already skeptical of the bear mauling story. So, remember, it's the whole force on the line, pal. Keep it in your pants." He called out to Marlon in warning before sitting back down in his patrol car.

Officer Marlon watched as Jacobs came and went without being much help, and he continued to catalog and mark the scene. He thought of Emily and the summers ago they had known each other. He tried to remember her face, and what she smelled like, and wondered if they would be the same.

Officer Marlon knelt down next to the severed arm of the teenage boy, and placed an evidence tag next to it. Then, he took a picture.

~ Officer Jacobs ~

The young officer Steven Jacobs turned off his patrol car as he parked outside the coroner's office waiting for the sheriff to arrive. His hands were shaking as he reached for the little bottle of Percocets that he had stolen from the punk in the alley. The afternoon was getting long, and he just wanted the day to be over so that he could enjoy his evening ritual of drowning himself in alcohol and falling asleep.

He still had one more item on his agenda for the day, and it had led him to a place he hated; the coroner. Jacobs popped the top off the little bottle and poured out some of the small tablets. After throwing three of them into his mouth, he laid his head back on the headrest and closed his eyes.

He started to daydream, like he did on occasion, of the little waitress that worked at the diner. He had always wished he could start a conversation with her, but had never had the courage. Instead, he would sit in his normal patrol spot in the parking lot across from the diner and watch her while she worked.

"Ah, Betty." He muttered aloud, swimming in his daydream.

Suddenly, Officer Jacobs snapped out of his fantasy at the sound of gravel crunching under incoming tires to see Sheriff Sanders pulling into the parking lot next to him.

Jacobs scrambled to hide the pills that were lying in the seat next to him, throwing them hastily into his glove box. When he looked up, Emily was staring at him through her car window. In that moment, Jacobs could feel the drugs lightening him, and his head continued to swim a bit as he felt time distorting.

Before he knew it, Emily was tapping on his window.

"Are you coming?" Emily asked with an oddly twisted look on her face. Jacobs could only nod in response. Emily didn't give him a beat as she marched towards the coroner's office, and Jacobs scrambled out of the car after her.

He straightened his shirt, and re-assembled himself the best he could before taking a breath and opening the door.

"Wait up, Emily." Jacobs called down the long narrow corridor. The sterile white hall played tricks with his mind, and he could barely manage to keep from staggering behind her.

"It's Sheriff, or Sheriff Sanders. If you're going to tag along, try to keep up, will ya?" Emily dictated, pulling rank over the local officer.

"Sheriff." Jacobs corrected, "I just don't see why we need to see the body again." He shuttered as they walked at the thought of seeing the old farmer again.

"I knew the man, not real well, but he's just going to be laying there in pieces. Maybe a little better arranged, but I just don't like seeing old Tom that way, he was an alright man." Jacobs explained in stern opposition.

Emily stopped in her tracks at hearing Jacobs' protest and turned, halting the other officer as she stared up into his face intensely.

"Then, why are you here?" Emily interrogated. "Why not just stay in your cruiser eating pills and daydreaming?" Emily scolded him, letting Jacobs know that she had seen the bottle in the passenger seat, "Don't think I can't see how dilated your eyes are, officer."

Jacobs gulped, "It's not like that. They're for my anxiety." He managed out.

"I bet." Emily narrowed her eyes in disbelief. "If I lived in this god-forsaken town, I'd probably have anxiety, too. What with all the bear attacks." She seared out sarcastically.

"Yeah, well...you try watching your neighbors and townsfolk get slaughtered." Jacobs growled back, "Maybe if you weren't just a county enforcer, and actually understood the place, knew the people, you wouldn't judge it so harshly."

"Your town's a shit pit." Emily burned her eyes deeper into Jacobs, and it only made him more angry and his face twitch, but Emily didn't relent, "Are we done here?"

Jacobs growled, and turned to walk back to his patrol car with clenched fists. Emily smirked in victory as she continued back towards the coroner, and the slices of Tom Kirkland she would reinvestigate. She hoped the coroner's findings would give her more insight as to what may have caused such a brutal attack.

Jacobs slammed the door to his cruiser, and fumed. "Shit pit? Where does she get off?" He asked himself aloud, slamming his palms on his steering wheel.

Jacobs leaned over and retrieved the pill bottle from his glove compartment. He unscrewed the cap, and ate another few of the pills.

"If this place is a shit pit..." he munched, "...then, so is the rest of the world."

8

~ A Morbid Fascination ~

Donald Gunther, an older man and the only coroner in Bay City, greeted Emily as she approached the main doors to the exam room. He walked with a slight instep from an old injury he had sustained that had never healed quite right, and it made for an eerie approach. His voice was raspy and deep, which made him even more ominous.

"Hello, Sheriff Sanders. It is a pleasure to see you again." Donald's voice boomed out, "It has been a while, hasn't it?"

"It's never long enough, Don." Emily smiled, "Did you get him all over here?" She asked with a cocked brow as she looked past the large white suited doctor, and to the larger exam room.

"I believe I've managed quite the reconstruction. Would you care to see?" Donald offered with an extended arm, jutted out towards the direction of Emily's gaze. She nodded hesitantly in return.

"Yeah. I think so." Emily replied with an oddly intrigued but cautious look, and Gunther opened the exam room door.

As they entered, the body of farmer Kirkland sat behind a retractable curtained-off portion of the room, on a steel table under a sheet. Donald pulled the curtain back, and Emily approached the body on the table. She looked down at the sheet, but didn't dare move it herself.

"The crime scene was like an old gory horror movie; bits of him everywhere." Emily recalled as the Coroner walked around the table. "I've never seen anything like it."

"Yeah, this one's a slasher movie nerd's wet dream, for sure." Donald said with a creepily detached grin as he reached for the sheet, "A real Frankenstein job." The portly doctor's coat stretched around his stomach and bounced as he chuckled at himself. Then, he drew back the thin cloth that separated them from the visage of Tom Kirkland.

What Emily saw was a grotesque attempt at reconfiguring the old man.

"Holy shit." Emily blurted out, turning at the sight for a moment. "That's the best you could do, Don? He's still not all there, is he?." She asked as she tried to examine the mangled sight of the body on the table in front of her.

"Not entirely, no." Donald answered, seemingly insulted, "There are a few more containers on the table over there that I haven't finished putting back together with the rest of him. I've only had the body for a few hours. I'm good, but I'm not magic, Sheriff."

Emily recoiled and her skin shivered as she examined the stitched-together corpse, "What the hell does that to a person, doc?" She asked, almost rhetorically. She didn't think even Donald Gunther would know the answer to that question. She didn't think anyone would, and little part of her hoped she never found out.

"Something big." Donald replied in a bit of wonderment, "Something very big."

"Like a bear?" Emily asked coaxingly.

"Maybe bigger." The coroner motioned with hands as if to signal something very large, and Emily nodded in thought. As she stared at the dead man in front of her, Donald walked over to a table in the corner of the room and picked up a small glass jar and brought it back over to her.

"Even stranger. There's ooze." The large coroner stated dramatically, holding up the container.

"Ooze?" Emily asked subconsciously as she came out of her stare and looked towards the jar of purplish-black slime the doctor held. She didn't know what to make of it, to Emily the man could have been holding anything.

"Goop, Goo, Ooze, Slime, Sludge. I'm not sure" Donald carried on, "It's the strangest thing that I've ever seen." He continued, stirring the jar around in the air before sitting down on the table next to the body. Then, the coroner slid on a latex glove, and opened the jar.

When he stuck his hand in, the slime moved and attached to his finger. He squished the slime between his fingers as he held them up for Emily to see.

As Emily scrutinized the substance, she could tell that it was slowly moving around on Donald's finger, "I've sent a smaller sample to the lab in the city to see if they could analyze it." He explained, squeezing the small ball of slime.

"I don't see how you do this, Don." Emily said, looking at the dead body and the slime.

"I've been told it takes a morbid fascination." The doctor replied with an odd smile as he continued to eye the ooze. As intrigued as she was about the doctor's slime, Emily didn't understand what it had to do with the old farmer. Donald continued to play with the slime in amazement, but Emily's patience was starting to wear thin.

"What does this have to do with anything, doc?" Emily asked, interrupting Donald's fun.

Donald put the slime back in the jar, and returned it to the other table, "Well, it ain't coming from me." He said with his back turned to Emily, "You know, if the mayor or the police chief start wondering where you get your ideas from, but you see, there weren't any tracks at Kirkland's house, and there's the ooze. It could only be one thing." He said matter-of-factly as he turned back to look at Emily.

Emily listened intently. "What, Don?" She urged him to continue.

"They call it a spectral trail." He explained, "It's the slime they leave behind." Donald crossed his arms defensively as he leaned back against a countertop, "You know we've been visited, Emily." He declared in his ominous fashion. "I've been watching these specials on the documentary channel, and they talk about this kind of stuff. The lack of evidence, the massive inexplicable carnage, and this goo! I'm telling ya right now, it's aliens!"

Emily's face soured, and her impatience with the doctor began to return.

"Goddamnit, Don. You've got to be kidding me. You've got nothing." Emily huffed and lowered her shoulders.

Donald could tell Emily wasn't as amused by the idea as he was, and he stood up from his lean, unfolding his arms.

"It's just a theory, Sheriff." Donald tried to lighten his enthusiasm, but Emily was already turning to leave. Donald draped the sheet back over the body as he watched her walk away, "Hey, Emily...I'm not saying it was aliens. Emily..." Donald called out to the dejected officer as she left.

"Just call me when you get those results back." Emily waved back to Donald as the doors to the exam room closed behind her. Emily made her way back to her patrol cruiser in the parking lot, and sat back in the seat. She sighed as she relaxed in the chair, placing her hand on her forehead.

"I hate this town." She told herself.

Emily did hate Bay City, and the lazy coast ideas it represented. She hated the slow pace at which everything moved, and more than anything she hated incompetence; which Bay City wasn't short on supply of.

It wasn't that the way of things couldn't improve, but it was that no one in town really wanted them to, not that Emily could tell anyway. There had been a way about Bay City as long as she could remember; something dark that gripped at everyone.

People didn't thrive in this town, they merely survived, and those who got out were happy to do so.

9

~ An Erected Official ~

Emily watched through her windshield as Mayor Adkins sped by down the highway in his car with his cell phone pressed against his ear. She huffed, and decided that she wouldn't pursue the Mayor of Bay City for speeding charges. She had almost had enough of the town for one day, and ticketing a town official just didn't seem worth the hassle it would cause.

The mayor clutched the steering wheel with his free hand. The other gripped his phone tight.

"I know, governor." Adkins quivered out into the receiver, "I get that the deaths look suspicious." His voice quaked as he spoke, "Yes, I understand that death is a hard platform to run for re-election on, but I..." The mayor stuttered out, but was quickly cut off as he pulled the phone away from his ear to save it from the volume of the governor's voice.

Adkins did his best not to swerve as he drove one-handed while being berated from the other end of the electronic device. It had just become dark enough that the passing cars began to turn on their headlamps as they went by, but Adkins didn't have a free hand to share the courtesy.

"The kid was, I don't know, fifteen maybe." Adkins answered the governor, but the irate official only continued to yell at the lowly mayor of Bay City. "The little details won't matter. I'll handle it." Richard Adkins said sternly as he ended the call and put his phone on the dash, and just as he did, Wendy felt safe to pull her head from below the steering column.

"Are you in some kind of trouble, baby?" The local salon owner asked the mayor, wiping the side of her mouth with the back of her hand. Wendy Pottercorn had regularly been seeing Dick for months, but they were keeping their relationship informal from the town. Not that the mayor cared much, about anything, really.

"It's nothing you should be concerned with" Adkins forced out disappointingly. His relationship with her was a byproduct of a lack of population and two opportunistic personalities colliding. Wendy saw opportunity in the mayor, but Dick saw something else in Wendy.

"You just focus on driving, mister. You've been swerving a lot." Wendy mused as she sat back in the passenger seat. She titled down the visor and began to adjust her hair in the mirror. Adkins flipped on the headlights and put both hands on the wheel, gripping it tight in frustration.

"I've been driving just fine." Dick shot back crudely, but before Wendy could respond, the mayor's phone began to ring again. He quickly picked it back up, and answered, "Yeah, what is it?" Adkins asked as though he already knew the voice on the other end of the line. "What do you mean? Where's the product? Please tell me you have it."

Jay stood next to an old phone booth talking on his cell phone. He was still with Duck, but Teddy had also joined them. Teddy had caught up to them at the local mini-mart where they awaited the night's activities together. Duck sat on the curb tossing rocks into the street, and Teddy threw punches at the air to fill in the time they waited for Jay to finish his report.

"Yeah, I'm getting the product. I just had to find a new driver." Jay told Dick Adkins who awaited his explanation, "It's even a van. I can move it all in one load. We won't even need Tux, now." Jay continued trying to convince Adkins that nothing was amiss.

Duck stood and watched as Rando walked down the sidewalk and past them. He towered over them, and to Duck and Teddy he was an eerie sight, not that it would stop Teddy from acting out the wait he did. He tapped Duck on the shoulder with the back of his hand to get his attention.

"That's the weirdo from the ice cream store." He said, purposely loud enough for Rando to hear him. "I heard he's a real psycho. Touched a kid so hard he broke his arm, and then he punched the kid's mom! Right in the mouth. The cops even came and picked him up, and threw him in jail."

"How's he still out here walking the street?" Duck shot out, as Rando had made some distance further. Duck drew his hand back, still holding one of the rocks from the curb, and threw it at Rando, hitting him in the back. It didn't phase the large man who continued to disappear down the sidewalk.

"That dude is definitely on the spectrum. Seriously." Teddy said snidely, and Duck laughed as they returned their attention back to Jay.

"Can you tell your cop friends to back off," Jay grumbled into the phone, "We took some real heat this afternoon with one of the local PD. The prick tried to shoot us!" Jay's tone heightened as he re-lived his moment with Officer Jacobs from earlier that afternoon.

"Yeah!" Duck shouted out, but Jay motioned for him to keep quiet. Teddy tapped Duck again in the same manner, pulling his gaze to the diner door, where Betty Fowler was exiting from her second shift. Unfortunately for her, her path home would have her walk past the bored hooligan teens.

She still wore her apron, and was pulling the tie out of her hair to let it down as she began making her way towards them. Duck immediately seized at the sight of the pretty young girl walking their way, but Teddy started in on his usual cat calls and face-making.

"Woo hoo, those are some nice stalks you're growing, girly." Teddy motioned upwards with his hands as he ran out his tongue, wiggling it around his lips before slurping it back inside his mouth. "Wanna go for a ride? Me and you could have some real fun." Teddy started to walk alongside Betty as she passed by. Duck grinned as he eyed the leggy waitress, but couldn't bring himself to be as bold as Teddy.

"Nice Winnie the Pooh cosplay, asshole." Betty said bluntly, looking down at the lifted waist of Teddys shirt, showing his pudgy midsection. Teddy followed her eyes down to his torso, and immediately began pulling his shirt back down. When he looked back up, Betty had continued on, only holding up a single finger for an ending salutation.

Duck began to laugh as Teddy walked back over to him and Jay.

"What the hell does that even mean? Natural order of things..." Jay complained as he hung up his phone, and ended the call with the mayor. "Stupid old shits always have to make things more complicated than they should be."

Duck continued to laugh, until Jay slapped him in the back, "What the hell are you laughing at?"

Jay glared angrily at them until slightly relaxing his posture, "Come on nerds, we gotta scram and meet up with Darrin." Jay waved for Teddy to follow him, and Duck filed in next to him as they carried onward down the street.

"Can we stop by the ice cream shop?" Duck said randomly as they saw it across the road head. "I got the munchies real bad, like bad bad, real bad." Duck insisted, but Jay wasn't happy with the suggestion.

"What are you? Six years old? We don't have time for that stupid shit. We're already running behind." Jay commanded. Being the leader of their little troupe was a hard task. Teddy had been diagnosed with Attention Deficit Disorder, and had never been able to stay calm, and Duck wasn't exactly the brains of the operation.

Jay was older, but not by much, and that gave him command of the two other goons. Which he constantly used to his advantage.

"If we don't get that shit where it needs to go, we'll never find another buyer. Keep your heads on straight, you morons. We can't have any mistakes tomorrow." Jay continued to insist, knowing that this would be his last chance to make things right with the mayor, and finally get out from under his thumb.

Jay wanted to rid himself of the mayor, and all the other *old shits*.

10

~ No More Bedtime Stories ~

Skylar had built a fort out of his bed posts and blanket, and had been playing underneath for it the better part of the afternoon while Darrin kept playing his video games, but poked his head out to hear his brother trying to manage to take a shower. Skylar could hear him fumbling around in the bathroom as he hurried to get ready to leave.

Skylar went back under his blanket fortress, and picked up his *Liznormous* action figure and searched for its counterpart, *Mighty Thunder Ray*. He found the old toy hiding under his pillow, and it had seen better days. The paint was chipped, his cape was gone, and his joints had become stuck in their flying action pose, but none of that bothered Skylar. He still flew the figure around, punching the giant lizard.

"Ha Ha!" Skylar shouted out, emulating the hero's signature call, and collided the muscled blonde man into the toy in his other hand, tossing it aside as though the impact had caused the projection.

Suddenly, Skylar was interrupted as Darrin pulled back the top of his fort.

"Awe, man. It was just getting to the good part!" Skylar pouted out, tossing his hands to his sides on the bed.

"Oh yeah? What's the good part?" Darrin coaxed, having heard Skylar talk about the cartoon on several occasions, and also watching it himself growing up; however, Darrin would pretend like he hadn't, for Skylar's amusement.

"He...Well, he...Mighty Thunder...He comes down out of the sky! Then, he just hit the bad guy once, and boom! It's all over! He wins, and he flies away again!" Skylar explained as excitedly as he always did, "but I didn't get to that part, yet. He just hit the lizard."

"Well, he's got to fly off now. You gotta go to bed early tonight." Darrin told his little brother as he began to untie the blanket from the bed posts. Skylar laid down, and let Darrin drape the blanket over him. This was a normal routine for them ever since Darrin had taken custody, and Skylar had gotten used to going to bed early when Darrin needed to leave at night.

"Awe man..." Skylar protested, but only moderately, then situated himself beneath his sheets. "Darrin, why aren't there any real superheroes?" He asked, squinting his eyes shut as Darrin reached for the light switch.

"That's a good question." Darrin paused, thinking for a second to try to find the most satisfying answer he could. "I guess it's because there aren't any giant super villains like Liznormous, either. I think if the world needed a superhero, there would be one, but since there isn't, I guess there's nothing to be afraid of. Now, get some sleep." Darrin smiled and flipped the light switch. Skylar gripped his Mighty Thunder Ray figure and rolled over. "I'll be back before breakfast. Goodnight."

Darrin walked out grabbing his coat and keys. Skylar could hear the front door close behind him as he left.

"Ha ha! Goodnight Liznormous!" Skylar whispered, emulating his hero once again.

~ The Ice Cream Man ~

"This is the part...where the plot...thickens." Rando said in his gruff monotone, as he stared blankly ahead, talking to an apparent nothing in front of his countertop, "Like a sludge...or a slime...or even...ice cream!" He continued telling no one, "From here...the story really gets going."

Little Evan Balden watched on from the small candies aisle as the large man watched cartoons and talked to himself. He had seen Rando before, but had never been able to talk to him out of a sense of dread. For Rando, it was a frequent occurrence. His stout appearance and dark features made him stand out amongst the others in town, and Evan found it odd that this ogre of a person would work at the ice cream shop.

Tonight was going to be the night Evan talked to Rando. He just needed to warm up to the idea a little more, and so he continued to watch the large man behind the counter.

Rando had managed to find reruns of his favorite cartoon show, *Mighty Thunder Ray*, and would keep them on repeat on the large monitor overhead as he worked.

"Will our hero...save the day...tune in...next time."
Rando finished with a singular huff of a laugh. He had just
begun his evening shift, and it wasn't unusual for him to stay
later and help Granny close the shop down for the night. She
stayed in the back usually, and Rando worked out front doing
the arm work, scooping the little balls of cream that made the
kids of Bay City so happy.

"Who are you talking to?" Evan managed out, looking
up at the towering figure. Rando looked down over the
counter to see the skinny eight year old peering at him, and
both of their eyes widened at the sight of the other. For a
moment, neither could manage to say anything to the other,
but then Evan's eyes narrowed in impatience. "I heard you.
Just now, you were talking to someone."
Rando only continued to stare blankly at the kid as
silent moments passed.

"O.k." The huge bearded man growled down in his
normal gruff.

Evan huffed, "Whatever. Can I get a scoop of
chocolate?" He asked, now more settled, and slightly
disappointed that Rando didn't seem to want to talk more.

"O.k." Rando affirmed, grabbing the cold metal scoop
from the reservoir.

He then began making Evan's ice cream cone in an almost masterful fashion. Rando had become very practiced in his short time at Granny's and Bay City, at a variety of things, and scooping ice cream had become one of them.

When he was done, he handed Evan a work of chocolate art covered with sprinkles, and dripping with chocolate syrup. Evan was no longer disappointed and instead beamed a huge grin up at the maestro.

Rando kept his gaze on Evan who had begun to lick the cone, "Four dollars...please." He said, holding out his palm, and Evan shuffled with his free hand around in his pocket, pulling out the bills he needed, and then placed them in Rando's meaty paw, "Thank you." His low voice boomed out at Evan in a very trained manner as he punched in a very few buttons, opening the register to hold the bills.

Evan's muted voice had returned, and he could only nod before running out of the store with his oversized ice cream treat.

Rando went back to watching his cartoons.

11

~ In The Fish Hook ~

Jacobs was shooting his third game of pool, when Emily Sanders walked into the tavern and sat down next to Chief Crocker at the bar. Joseph wasn't expecting to see Emily at the nightly after hour meeting down at the Fish Hook; Bay City's only night life and watering hole for the local officials after a hard day's work. Rick, the bartender, noticed Emily's approach as he had always had a keen eye, and a good memory for repeat customers.

"Evening Sheriff." Rick called out, and Crocker turned to fully acknowledge Emily sitting beside him. Emily nodded to the bartender, and the rest of her local cohorts before Rick came over, wiping his hands clean with a rag. "The usual, Emily?"

"Yeah, that sounds good, Rick. How have you been?" Emily asked, confirming her order.

"It's a full house tonight. I can't complain." The Fish Hook's resident ale pourer grabbed a pint glass and began to pour a draft beer for Emily. Emily looked around the room again, noticing that a lot of the locals were indeed in attendance. Rick grabbed a small shot glass and poured a shot of bourbon into it, and handed both drinks to the sheriff.

Emily grabbed the shot, and dropped it into the pint. The beer splashed and fizzed as the two beverages mixed. Then, after letting the drink settle for a second, Emily picked up the pint glass and tilted it back, sliding the liquid into her mouth.

"It's been that kind of day, Emily." Joseph said with widened eyes as he watched the little woman drink the stiff drink. Emily's glass clanked against the bar as she returned it empty. She held up her hand to Rick.

"Thanks, Rick. Let's do that one more time." Emily requested, before turning to stare the police chief in the face, "Yeah, Joey. It's been that kind of day." Rick repeats his previous routine, and in moments delivers Emily a second round of drinks.

"I take it things didn't go so great with Donald over at the morgue?" Crocker asked with unmasked curiosity. He knew better than anyone that Emily wasn't going to give up without getting all the details, but he also knew this case wasn't a regular one. He didn't expect her to have found much.

"Screw you, Chief." Emily shot back quick and angry as she mixed and drank her strong second serving, "I know you just want me to put a bow on this, but you know where I sit." It wasn't taking very long for the alcohol to take effect on Emily, and she had always been a verbose drunk.

"You screw yourself, Sheriff." Chief Crocker replied with a downturned grin. He was sick of Emily sticking her nose where he didn't think it belonged, and he had already drank a few beers before she had arrived, relaxing his decorum. "If you just came in here to berate me or the other guys about this case, you can just leave. We don't come here to talk shop." Joseph took a swig of his beer.

A loud bang broke the tension when a cue ball smacked against the bar next to Emily, and bounced to a halt under her stool. Her shoulders shot up as the bar got quiet.

"Hey Emily! You mind handling..." Officer Jacobs hiccuped mid sentence, "Handing my ball back." Jacobs laughed an intoxicated and loud laugh, and Brad Taylor, another officer in the Bay City Police force, began to laugh along with him.

Furious, Emily leaned down and grabbed the solid pool ball and hurled at the two local officers, sending it crashing against the wall behind them with an even louder bang than the first. The whole tavern remained quiet as they watched the exchange.

"What the hell, Emily!" Jacobs protested as he fetched the ball.

"That one's a few kernels short of a cob, if you asked me." Emily said, turning back to the police chief, "You're lucky he hasn't burnt the station down."

"Relax, Emily." Joseph insisted, "He's just messing around. After the past couple of weeks, we all need a little R and R. You know what I mean?" The police chief explained, knowing the Sheriff would know about the previous case with the Murphy family's son. It had also been a supposed animal mauling with the teenage boy's body found in the woods, and the previous chief had resigned over the case.

"Running from your problems isn't going to fix them, and neither is hiding in here drinking yourselves stupid just because a punch card said you can." Emily scolded, but it only made Joseph roll his eyes in dispute. Emily had started slurring as she gave her speech, letting him know that she was feeling her drink. "Are you even listening, chief?"

"No. Not really, Emily." Crocker said as he got up from this stool, grabbing his own drink and turning to walk towards the back lounge area of the tavern, leaving Emily behind. The lone Sheriff sat by herself in a huff at the bar.

"By this time tomorrow, I'm going to have found out what murdered Tom Kirlkand, Chief. Bear, or no bear!" She yelled at Joseph's back as he made his way inside the video poker room. There, a little old woman sat at his favorite machine.

Joseph let out a grunt as he stood obnoxiously close to the lady at the game. At first she didn't take the hint, and continued to play her round at the machine.

"Do you mind?" Crocker growled out gesturing his thumb to the next game over. The little woman's eyes widened as he fumed, and eventually complied.

"Excuse me." She snarked out, tilting her nose slightly as she changed to the next poker machine. Crocker sat down on the little stool and pulled out a five dollar bill. He never played for a lot of money, but then again, Joseph Crocker didn't really have a lot of money. He pressed the button, and the reels began to spin.

The door chimed as officer Roger Marlon walked into the Fish Hook. He noticed Emily sitting alone at the bar, but was greeted by the rest of the patrol as he entered.

"Hey! Marlo!" Taylor shouted towards the door, and Rick and the rest of the bar turned with a raised glass to greet him. Roger started to join Jacobs and Taylor at the pool table, but not before seeing Rick at the bar for a drink. The old barkeep nodded to the younger uniformed officer.

"Are you still on duty, officer?" Rick asked, eyeing the patrolman's attire.

"I got back and the station was empty. I figured I'd find everyone here." Marlon noted as he scanned around the room, "How do you put up with these assholes, Rick?" Marlon laughed as he nodded towards Jacobs.

"That's why I've always got the rag in my hand." Rick snorted out as he wiped the bartop, "What are you having?"

"Just a beer, Rick. Keep it cheap." Marlon responded with a grin, and Rick nodded and turned to reach into the cooler behind him. Marlon leaned over and turned his gaze to Emily, who sat a few seats away. She noticed him looking in her direction and caught eyes with the patrolman. "Emily." Officer Marlon nodded.

"Officer Marlon." She said in curt reply.

"Oh come on, Emily. I've been meaning to call you." Roger Marlon's demeanor broke in a single sentence as he tried to explain. "It's just that the past month or so has been really hectic. You can understand, right?" Silence ensued as Sheriff Sanders stared blankly at the quivering and desperate man explaining himself as he moved down a stool towards her.

Rick sat down an unimpressively inexpensive lager on the bar for Marlon, and smiled. Emily saw the beverage and rolled her eyes. Marlon twisted off the cap in a defiant sarcastic fashion in response to her disinterest.

"Relax, shithead. I'm not here for you." Emily stated blunt and loose. Then, she got up from her stool and went back to the video poker lounge to catch up with the police chief. Marlon sighed as Emily walked away, grabbing his beer and getting up from his seat. Emily nudged her way into the video poker lounge, and sat herself back down beside the unamused Joseph Crocker.

"You do know these things are rigged, don't ya?" Emily nosed over at Joseph's machine, "Oh sure, it will let you win a little, but just so you keep playing."

Crocker huffed, irritated by the continuing interruption that Emily Sanders had decided she was entitled to, but chose to ignore her and continue playing. Emily's brow narrowed at the dismissal, and she placed her hand over the display.

"Come on, Joey! You expect me to believe this whole bear mauling bullshit?" Emily raised her voice as she looked down at the seated interim police chief. "There's been no sightings from hunters in years, and now what? Now, you say you've got a killer bear running around dismembering old ranchers and killing kids in the woods?"

The woman at the video poker game behind Emily gasped at what she overheard, and Crocker could hear it. It appalled him that Emily was so open about the case in public, and it wore down his patience with her. His eyes glared up at the sheriff, but he stayed seated.

"I don't know what to tell you, Emily." The chief said low and slow, before becoming more vibrant, "Maybe..." he paused unnecessarily, "It was just a goddamned hungry cougar or mountain lion."

"It didn't eat anything, not a bite of either one of them, Chief." Emily scowled harder, and Joseph stood to meet her eye to eye, "I read over the Murphy kid's report before I came to Bay City, and it didn't look anything like what I saw at Don's this afternoon when he showed me Kirkland's body."

"What are you trying to say, Sheriff?" Crocker huffed out.

"The department you took over hadn't had any serious cases in more than fifteen years, and now you've had two animal maulings inside a month. If it were the same animal, like a bear, it would be the same report; at least similar. These two reports look like two different animals, entirely." Sanders insisted, trying to get the police chief to confirm her suspicions.

"Maybe it was two different animals." Crocker said glaring into Emily, who remained rather unfazed by his attempt to dominate her. Joseph could tell his bravado did little to aid him in evading her interrogation. "Damnit, Emily. Why are you digging on this so hard?" He asked, trying to lighten his tone.

Emily peered around the lounge and tavern hall. She watched as everyone laughed and drank, all happy to have the night to do so. Rick filled glasses, and tourists ate the fried clams and butter-dipped crab, losing their worries by the beach. Everyone seemed so care-free, smiling, and didn't have a concern about the deaths, drugs, and debauchery that plagued their sleepy town. It was as if they didn't know their town was covered in darkness. Emily could see it, but it didn't seem like they could; like it was all an act these people played.

"Something is going on here." Emily muttered out to herself, "I can feel it."

"What's that, Emily?" Crocker asked in earnest, not hearing Emily's murmur. He looked around to try to see what Emily saw, but like the rest of them, he was also blind to the darkness that surrounded him.

"I think this might just be a little too big for your department to handle, right now." Emily stated boldly and bluntly to the fresh police chief, whose face immediately turned back to frustration.

"We were just fine until you showed up, Sheriff." Crocker fumed, "It's not like you're some holy Jesus neither." He nodded to his glass as he swilled a large gulp imitating her at the bar, only he wasn't able to fit the entire volume into his mouth and the extra spilled out from the sides and down his face. Emily recoiled at the sight, making a disgusted face at him in return.

Emily turned to look away from Crocker, but in doing so locked eyes with Marlon, who had been watching her from the pool table.

"You're an idiot." Emily stated plainly, almost to herself, again. "I'm going to go and let you get cleaned up." She looked down at the pool of beer on the floor, but Crocker just laughed as she turned and left the little video poker lounge, then returned to his game.

~ Rack 'Em ~

"You're up, Rodge." Jacobs called out, breaking Roger's glance at Emily, "Remember, you're stripes!" Jacobs let out a small laugh as he nodded to the table to show Roger Marlon what he was up against. When Marlon turned and saw the pool table, he sighed. All the striped balls were still on the table, and he was losing, not that he was paying much attention to their game.

"Come on, man. Just shoot already." Jacobs urged arrogantly, wanting to hurry to his next shot.

"I was just thinking." Roger replied as he chalked his cue and walked around the table looking for his best shot, 'We got that call earlier from the RV park manager." Marlon bent over, and lined up his stick with the cue ball, and with a sudden clack the balls raced around the table until two of his striped balls fell into opposite corner pockets.

"Anyone ever go and check that out?" Marlon asked the two other officers. Both of them were more intent on playing the pool game now that Roger had managed to make his first shot.

"Nah, wrote that off as a private incident. No evidence of a crime being committed or anything, just Geoff being nosy, again." Taylor admitted, bringing his beer bottle to his lips with a slight shrug. Marlon lined up for his next shot.

"Didn't he say he saw blood on an RV?" Marlon asked, snapping his stick back and into the cue again. Another striped ball landed in a side pocket, and Marlon looked back up to the two officers watching him from the other end of the table.

"Nah, he said he saw some couple cleaning what looked like blood from their RV, but he said he couldn't be sure. Just that the couple was acting weird, but you know Geoff...He acts weird, so..." Jacobs chimed in. "At the time, we didn't think it would amount to much, and it's been a busy day. Chances are, even if we did go over there, we would just be taking a statement, and with everything else that's been going on, I didn't think we needed the paperwork."

Marlon rolled his eyes at the comment. "Yeah, Geoff's a little off, but if he said he saw something, we might need to go check it out." Marlon continued to take his shots at the game, not missing one. Taylor watched in amazement, but Jacobs had become less thrilled.

"What, you want to go, now?" Jacobs raised his tone, irritated by both the concept of having to work and the fact that his easy win was now in jeopardy as Roger quickly caught up to his last ball.

"Why not?" Marlon smiled, pulling back the pool stick once again. He eyed down the easy line he left himself on the eleven ball, and just next to it, the eight ball. With the right geometry Roger would be able to hit his ball into the last one ricocheting both into opposite corner pockets.

"Geoff's a night owl. He keeps the park open late for stragglers. He'll still be up, and we'll find out what he really saw." Marlon drew back once more, and with little effort accomplished the difficult angle, hurling the eleven into the eight ball and bouncing it into the closer pocket. The black ball followed quickly dropping into the other corner. "Besides, this game is over." Roger smiled victoriously, and laughed as he saw the unexpectedly defeated look on Jacobs.

"What the hell?" Jacobs shot out, but seemed more stunned than upset.

"Are you ready to go?" Marlon asked, but just as he did he noticed Emily walking towards them. Her eyes locked with his, and Marlon's mind paused in mid-thought.

"Wait, are you guys talking about the dead bike kid? You think he was hit by an RV?" Taylor asked, but his back was turned and he didn't notice the Sheriff's approach behind him. Jacobs' eyes widened as he noticed Sanders hear the patrolman, and cock her head to the side in curiosity.

"Shit, Taylor. You could have just kept your mouth shut." Jacobs whispered loudly amongst the group. Emily cut her eyes towards Jacobs, obviously hearing him, too. Officer Taylor turned and saw Emily standing behind him and jumped back a step.

"On the video game!" Taylor shouted at Emily. "You see, we all play this game, and there's a dead kid on a bike, and we're just talking about a video game, right?..." Taylor tried to quickly lie to cover their topic of conversation, but was too intoxicated to be convincing and Marlon and Jacobs knew it.

Emily knew it, too.

"Not buying it, officer. You got another body now, don't you?" Emily steamed out. Marlon and Jacobs both stared blankly at the Sheriff, until Jacobs took a step back behind Roger to shield himself from the Sheriff's interrogation. "When did it happen?"

"I got the call this afternoon. I arrived on scene at the highway, and the body was already cold. Hit and run, not a mauling." Marlon explained, "It was an unrelated case, and we didn't see a need to brief the county until the case was closed." He stated with a professional blunt tone that Emily did not appreciate.

"You could have said something earlier, asshole." Emily peered around Officer Marlon to scold Jacobs, then drew her angered gaze back to Roger, "and if I'm in town, I'm involved. You notify me immediately of any deaths or arrests." Emily's voice pitched up a little and Officer Taylor reached out and put his hand on Emily's shoulder to try to calm her.

"Calm down, Emily. It was a simple mistake." Taylor said with a drunken grin, "We weren't trying to hide anything, promise." He massaged his fingers into her shoulder to try to sooth her as he talked, and Emily became incensed. "We're all friends here, Emily." Taylor spoke with an obnoxiously over-emphatic tone, and Marlon knew what was about to happen.

Emily's thumb and forefinger clasped around Taylor's groping hand, and with little more than a twist of her wrist, Emily spun the man to the bar floor. Then, her boot landed with a thud against his chest as she pulled on his hand. Taylor howled. "You keep your hands off of me, you filthy jerk."

"That's enough, let him go." Jacobs stepped forward again to try to aid his friend, the bar now looking on as an audience. Emily twisted her hand a little harder, and Taylor howled in pain, again.

Jacobs reached forward to grab Emily's arm to pull Taylor free from her grip, but Emily released Taylor just before, moving her posture and punching Jacobs in the jaw, sending him to the floor as well. Taylor used the opportunity to scurry away, but Emily leaned down over Jacobs and was about to start pummeling him.

Before she could, Officer Marlon wrapped his arms around the much smaller sheriff and pulled her back.

"That's enough, Sheriff." He said softly into Emily's ear. She continued to struggle for a moment, before realizing that she couldn't free herself from Roger's arms. Jacobs backed away holding his hand to his jaw before standing back up at a safe distance.

"What is your problem, Emily?" Jacobs whined as Marlon held Emily tight.

"Let me go, Roger." Emily demanded in a less intense volume, and after a moment of Emily's surrender, the officer released her.

"My problem is that prick. He's an idiot." Emily glared at Jacobs, and Roger didn't understand why, but he knew that Emily couldn't be around Officer Jacobs without becoming angry at him.

Marlon looked to Jacobs, who was now nursing his bruised ego and rubbing his wound.

"You go ahead without me." He told Jacobs, "I'll catch up with you in the morning."

"Fine." Jacobs agreed in protest, "but it was your idea in the first place." He turned, grabbing his coat from the bar chair next to the pool table, and proceeded to leave the tavern in an angered fume. Emily relaxed a little more after Jacobs had left, and Taylor hid over at the bar. Marlon looked at her in confusion.

"What the hell do you have against Jacobs?" He asked abruptly.

"I just don't like him, Roger." Emily said in a much calmer demeanor, "He's not a good cop."

Roger sighed, knowing what Emily said wasn't a stretch to believe, but also didn't judge his coworkers the way that she did. To Roger, everyone had their own problems, and whatever Jacobs' were, they were his business.

He never pried, and that made it easier for him to turn a blind eye.

12

~ A Night at the Park ~

Officer Jacobs turned off the lights on his patrol cruiser as he pulled to a stop in the parking lot of the old Bay City RV Park. It had been there as long as anyone in the town could remember; always changing ownership. One person would come to town and buy it with the hopes of making it a waypoint on some tourist map, but so far that had never happened, and it had become home to the less fortunate of Bay City's inhabitants.

The new owner was much like the others, but instead of selling off the park once he got bored, he employed Geoff, the park's manager for the last few years.

Jacobs knew Geoff from a few incidents he had been called to settle at the RV park, and Geoff usually kept to himself in his old camper, but tonight the office light was still on. Jacobs made his way around to the side door, where he was greeted by Geoff holding a baseball bat.

"It's about damn time!" Geoff shouted at the patrolman, as he held open the store's door. Geoff was already in his pajamas and tee shirt, but was still working the office, "I called you guys earlier this morning...well, they're back!" Geoff's hand pointed to one of the RV's in the lot.

"What's up with the bat, Geoff?" Jacobs asked, noticing Geoff's frantic demeanor.

"Who knows what the hell these people have done! I'm not going to be next...I have to defend myself!" Geoff urged, shaking the bat in the air. "They're killers, I tell ya!"

Jacobs smirked, not giving Geoff much credit to his story, "O.k. Geoff, you wait here, I'll go check it out." Geoff grimaced at the officer..

"They're in spot seven." Geoff growled out, "Be careful. They were being really loud."

Jacobs nodded, and proceeded to make the minor trek to spot seven in the RV park. Along the way he could begin to hear the two loud voices of a couple arguing. Dave and Marta hadn't been able to leave Bay City and had returned for another night's stay at the park, and neither were very happy about the change in plans.

"Why did you have to use the shirt I bought you on our honeymoon?" Marta demanded an answer while holding the red stained shirt. "You knew it was blood you were wiping off, and blood stains, David." She continued as she fumed.

"Calm down, Marta!" Dave commanded, "It didn't fit me any more anyway." He grumbled as he flipped through the channels on the tv tuner trying to find the sports channel. He gripped the remote control tight and mashed the buttons in anger, fed up with his wife. His eyebrows pressed hard against his nose as he peered into the screen, flipping.

"You said it was your favorite shirt!" Marta steamed out, crossing her arms. "Is that how you're going to feel about me? Are you just going to use me up, and throw me out when I don't fit anymore? Is that what's happened, David?" She scolded over Dave's shoulder, getting louder and louder.

"Oh dear god, Marta, just please shut up." Dave turned, yelling back at Marta, but holding the remote to the television and increasing the volume.

"Why?" Marta huffed, "Can get it loud enough to tune me out?"

"Damnit, Marta!" Dave growled and pressed the power button on the remote, turning off the little television.

He stood walking back into the back of the RV around Marta. "You're not even talking about anything. What? Some stupid shirt got ruined." He groaned as he passed.

"Some stupid shirt?" Marta questioned loudly in protest, "Some stupid shirt!" She yelled as she threw the stained shirt against Dave's back. "I'm not the one who used it to wipe blood off my RV because I hit someone! All because you don't like wearing your glasses!" Marta screamed as she clenched her fists by her sides, "Some stupid shirt!"

Dave turned back to face Marta. Both of them were the most angry they had ever been as they glared into each other's eyes, firmly unmoved by the other.

"I said, shut the hell up, Marta." Dave said slowly in an ominously dark tone.

"Who does that, David?" Marta blurted out, ignoring David's change in demeanor. "Who just keeps on driving and doesn't look back? You keep saying it was a deer, but it wasn't a deer, was it, David?" Marta had become hysterical in her accusation; stomping her foot into the floor of the motorhome as she leaned closer into Dave's face.

With a sudden clasp of his hand, Dave grabbed Marta by the arm. His hand squeezed as he gripped her and pulled her closer to bring his other palm into her cheek. The sound of the smack echoed through the camper, and sent Marta to the floor, but Dave didn't let go. Instead, he climbed on top of Marta, mounting her, and brought his hand back up for a second round.

"I keep telling you to shut up!" Dave shouted as he slapped Marta again, turning her face towards the camper door. Her eyes began to well up with tears, and she could do nothing to fight back. Dave was much bigger than Marta.

"Stop!" Marta cried out with blood in her teeth, but Dave wasn't listening to her anymore. Marta's head bounced against the floor as Dave turned her cheek a third time. Spit dripped from his seething lips and he grasped his hands around Marta's throat and began to squeeze.

Marta gagged, and her hands gripped his trying to pull them away, when suddenly the camper door burst open.

"Get off of her!" Officer Jacobs yelled into the motorhome with his flashlight shining into Dave's face. "Sir, you have two seconds!" Jacobs pulled up his sidearm and aimed it at Dave.

Dave jumped back, coming to his senses, but pointed down on the floor to a writhing Marta.

"It was her!" Dave yelled. "She made me!"

"Ma'am, can you move?" Jacobs called out to Marta, still keeping his weapon focused on Dave. Dave began to panic and rock back and forth, looking for a way to escape. Marta nodded to the officer, and began to pull herself out through the camper door past Jacobs.

Once she was out, Marta stood and dusted herself off, coughing a little bit as she did.

"Screw you, David." Marta yelled back into the camper from the safety of the patrolman's back.

"Sir, come out of the camper, slowly." Jacobs commanded, flicking his pistol in the direction he wanted Dave to follow.

"No way!" Marta shouted, "I'm not sticking around this loser any more. I'm out of here!" She began to walk back down the gravel path that led back to the park office.

"Don't listen to a word that bitch says." Dave declared as he stepped down out of the motorhome. "She's as looney as they come. She don't know a damned thing."

"Sir, calm down, and turn around. I'm going to need to cuff you while I look around your vehicle." The officer instructed Dave.

"What? I haven't done anything?" Dave insisted, ignoring what the officer had walked in seeing him doing. Dave hesitated, but he eventually let the patrolman latch the handcuffs around his wrists. Marta had made it a decent distance away, and ignored the office as she left the park grounds on foot down the highway.

Geoff watched as Marta left, and turned to see the officer arresting Dave. He gripped at his bat nervously as he kept looking through the window.

Then, as it does from time to time on the coast, it began to rain.

~ It Came From Below ~

The moonlight glistened through the treeline that surrounded the park and spanned down the long highway road. The light drops dripped down from the dark clouds above, and Marta's feet splashed along in the newly forming puddles. She held the side of her face as she ran, not distinguishing tears from the rain.

"I can't believe that asshole hit me." Marta muttered to herself in sobbing anger as she continued down the side of the road. She found it odd that she hadn't seen a single car pass by since she had started her journey, but she did notice that the wind had picked up and she wrapped her arms around her body for warmth.

The leaves rustled across the asphalt and an eerie whistle sang through the air. The darkness made Marta start to feel nervous and wish she hadn't left. She thought about turning back, but just as she stopped to mull over the decision, a noise came from the bushes on the other side of the road.

The loud sound snapped Marta's attention to the dim lit forestry on the roadside.

"What was that?" She asked, trying to manage a voice above a whisper. She had left her purse and all her belongings back at the camper, and had no way of seeing the figure that emerged across her path; however, she could tell something was there.

The shadow crept across the blacktop as the rain picked up. Marta began to run back the way she came, and she could hear the creature behind her. It was big. It squished as it dripped along the street following the middle-aged woman, leaving a trail of black slime as it slithered.

Marta dashed through the raindrops, but she felt the shadow get closer and closer. She didn't dare turn back to see the thing, but she could hear the sound of steam coming from behind her as she ran. Marta's eyes squinted shut as she pushed for more speed, and she ran as fast as she ever had.

As she reached the RV park sign, Marta suddenly stopped hearing her pursuer. She huffed, and slowed down, turning back to see if she had made it to safety. The park office was only a few dozen yards away, and she could see the lights of Officer Jacob's patrol car as she rounded the last little grove of trees. Marta saw nothing behind her, only the empty dark asphalt.

Marta came to a stop, confused. She investigated every direction, wondering what it was that was just chasing her.

Then, she started to feel very disappointed in herself, telling herself that she had imagined whatever it was.

Marta turned back to the office as she heard the faint sound of the bell ringing as Geoff came back outside. She started to walk again, waving to Geoff to get his attention, but he was still watching Jacobs inspect the motorhome. The blue and red lights illuminated the little patch of darkness that held the RV park, and Dave stared out from the back window of the officer's cruiser.

He could see Marta walking towards Geoff and the office, and he frantically began tapping on the glass.

"Holy shit!" Dave screamed in terror, "Marta! Look out!" He yelled, but his voice was muted by the window. He began beating his cuffed hands against the backglass. "Marta!"

Geoff noticed Dave, but didn't understand what he was doing. He watched for a moment, and noticed that Dave was looking past him, and turned to see Marta walking towards him, and behind Marta was a creature unlike anything Geoff's mind could comprehend.

"Oh my god!" Geoff's finger shot forward as he shouted, "What the hell is that thing!"

Its eyes shined through the thicket of trees that could barely hide it. Steam rose from the treetops as it stood, hulkingly massive in the grove. Ooze dripped off from its sinewy tentacle-like appendages. All that Marta could see when she turned was rows of jagged fangs the creature held in its maw. Her eyes widened at the sight of the beast.

"Run!" Geoff screamed, but Marta was frozen in place. Jacobs heard Geoff, and came back around the camper to see the scene.

The monster moved slowly out from the little patch of forest, and as the rain hit the creature steam rose from its oily black skin. Its arm descended and as it did, it dropped its gnarled and large pincer, dripping slime to the ground.

Without a second's notice, the creature flung its claw through the air, stretching its arm like a whip, and impaled Marta through the forehead. Then, it plucked out its appendage and retracted it back. Marta fell face first into the gravel, and a pool of blood began to form around her head.

The monster howled into the night sky, its teeth rumbling in its massive open mouth. Geoff gripped the baseball bat tight in his hands, and a mortified Jacobs began sneaking back to his cruiser, trying not to be seen by the creature.

"Well!" Geoff screamed out as moisture ran down his forehead. "Come get some of this, you piece of shit!"

The beast's attention turned to Geoff immediately, and without hesitation the creature leaped towards the park manager, covering the long distance easily as it dropped sludge along the path. As Geoff pulled back the bat to swing, the monster's jaw opened and enveloped him, grinding him down with its sharp rows of long piercing teeth.

"Let's get the hell out of here!" Dave yelled at Officer Jacobs as he got into the car, and Jacobs slammed the door shut and began to fumble with the keys and controls, turning on the siren. The creature began to move quickly towards the sound, dripping slime from its body as it launched itself at the patrol car, crushing in its roof.

Jacobs and Dave began to scream as the metal crunched above them. Ooze ran down the windows covering their view of the outside. The car jostled back and forth as the monster gripped into it from above, until the passenger door broke open. Jacobs crawled along the front seats trying to make it to the open door.

"You can't just leave me!" Dave yelled through the metal mesh divider. Jacobs looked back to Dave, but said nothing, and continued his escape through the other side of the car.

The creature ripped up the roof of the patrol car, tearing it like a can opener, and pulled out Dave with its long clawed arm.

Jacob's wide eyes watched as he ran aimlessly towards a camper parked at the other end of the lot. The creature's grip pulled at Dave's limbs, tearing them off one by one, and it howled again. Jacobs gulped as he ran to the camper door.

He pounded and pounded, "Police, open up!"

"What?" an old woman's voice came through the thin metal door. "Excuse me? Did you say, 'police'?" She asked slowly.

"Yes!" Jacobs looked back at the large slimy monster tearing apart his car, "It's an emergency! Let me in!" His panicked voice called back.

"Do you have a warrant?" The woman asked, and Jacobs could hear her coming to the door.

He pulled his sidearm as he pressed his body against the camper, waiting for the old woman to open the door.

"No ma'am. I just need to come inside. Please!" He urged, but his fearful voice shook and made the woman nervous, and he could hear her footsteps stop.

The creature held its deformed head in the air, sniffing, searching for Jacobs.

"No warrant, no dice! I'm watching my shows! Come back later!" She declined, but Jacobs pounded on her door again. His hand twitched with his finger on his firearm.

"Ma'am!" He called out, louder now. "I really need you to open this door, now!" The monster turned in his direction, seeing him with its shining eyes. Jacobs began to pound obnoxiously. "Ma'am!"

The old woman came to the door, pulling it open angrily. "Goddamn it! What?" her irritated voice shot out through the screen. Jacobs grabbed the screen door, and pushed the woman aside to get into the camper. She saw his uniform and firearm first, "What the hell?", but then looked out at the park to see the creature coming towards her.

The woman jumped in shock at the sight of the thing, and slammed the door shut.

"What the hell is that thing?" She asked the cowering policeman who stood in her wet-head. Jacobs could only shrug unknowingly as he clutched his pistol. "Well, are you going to use that thing?" She asked, and Jacobs only shrugged again.

The small camper began to shake as the monster latched onto it with its claw. It pulled the flimsy front door from the motorhome and flung it across the park.

"Give me that." She demanded, sticking out her hand for Jacob's gun. He nodded, and quickly handed it over.

Rita, a bus driver for the local school district, and divorced mother of two, leaned out from the camper entrance and aimed at the monster. She yelled as she squeezed, sending a volley of bullets into the creature's body. The metal chunks splattered pieces of the sludge creature's body onto the ground, but didn't seem to faze it. She fired again, and again, but the monster still advanced.

It threw its tentacled claw, running it through the gunwoman, and pinning her to the back wall of her camper. The gun flew from her hand, and landed on the floor in front of Jacobs. The claw retracted once more, and Jacobs dove for his firearm as Rita fell to the floor next to him, lifeless.

Jacobs crawled to the wall next to the door, and slid up to a stance, trying to peer around the doorframe.

He pulled up his weapon, ready to aim, and stepped out around the corner to confront the creature. It was right in front of him, and he pushed the barrel into the creature's body. Slime ran down onto his hands as he stared deep into the maw of the beast.

Jacobs squeezed, but the clip was empty.

13

~ The Mourning After ~

Emily turned in the sheets of Roger Marlon's bed as he was suddenly startled awake by his phone. Its loud ring pinged off the walls making it echo through his small mid-town apartment. Roger snapped up from his bed, and reached for his phone. Emily, feeling her head aching from the previous night, decided to pretend she was still asleep.

The sunlight was just starting to pour in through a crack in the blinds, and it shined directly in Emily's face keeping her awake.

"Marlon." Roger said, seeing the Bay City Police Department number on the caller I.D. "What?!" Officer Marlon said in shock, a little too loud for the morning, and Emily could no longer pretend she wasn't where she was. "How many? Holy shit! Nevermind, I'm on my way." Roger hung up the phone and returned it to his night stand as he got out of bed.

Officer Marlon began to dart around his apartment, dressing himself in yesterday's uniform in a hurry, and Emily became alarmed.

"I didn't think you worked the morning shift?" She asked, as Roger strapped his belt and holster around his waist.

"Not usually." He replied in a panicked rush, "Where's your phone?" He asked, putting on his shoes. "There's been another incident. A bad one. Chief is trying to get a hold of you."

Emily looked around for a moment, until she found her jacket next to the bed, and pulled out her phone. The battery had depleted overnight, and it wouldn't turn on.

"It's dead." She huffed as she threw the device onto the comforter she was still under.

Marlon paused in his stride, and gave Emily an oddly serious look. Emily couldn't help but notice that Roger's face struggled to stay calm, and it was as if the man wanted to break down in front of her.

"What's happened, Roger?" Emily asked.

"Multiple homicides at the RV park." Marlon muttered out. "We've lost a man. It's Jacobs." He explained with a nervous stutter. Emily's eyes widened, and she couldn't believe what she was hearing. "Everyone at the park..." Roger tried to get out, "They're all..." He stopped mid-sentence and grabbed the keys to his patrol car from the table beside the door.

"Emily, I've got to go." He said, grabbing the door handle.

Emily slid out of the bed, wrapping herself in the sheet as she began to hastily find her clothes, "I'm right behind you! Go!" Roger nodded, and quickly left through the door as Emily began to put on her uniform. She noticed the clock on the wall, and it was later in the morning than she had imagined, almost ten o'clock.

"Shit." Emily griped aloud, rushing to find her badge and sidearm.

Emily made her way out of the small loft apartment, and out on the bright late morning street. There, she saw some of the town's teens leaning against the window to the ice cream store. She would have to make her way past them to get back to where she had to park her cruiser, and along the way she noticed Darrin standing among the local boys.

"Ah ha ha," Duck pointed at the Sheriff, "Looks like someone's doing the walk of Shane!" He laughed out as he eyed the female officer. Darrin slapped the back of his arm against Duck to shut him up. Jay chuckled, but covered his mouth to keep Emily from seeing. It didn't stop her from hesitating at the comment and the sight of Darrin.

"What did you just say?" Emily asked the ratty-looking teenage boy. Duck started to repeat himself, but Darrin stepped forward with his crutch.

"He didn't say anything, ma'am. Just being a stupid kid." Darrin soothed out in a militaristic fashion, and Emily peered back and forth at Duck and Jay, not liking the company that she found Darrin in.

"Everything alright here, Darrin?" She asked as she watched both of the other two boys hold back their demented laughter at the situation. Jay wanted to burst, and Duck was enjoying having Darrin cover for him. Emily began to lose her patience with the teens, and needed to continue on to the RV park, almost not letting Darrin answer her question.

"Everything's fine here, L.t. I can handle these two idiots." Darrin mused with a grin as he urged Emily onward to her destination. She merely nodded an eye at Darrin to imply she was watching him, but then proceeded to the small parking garage that held her car.

Once the sheriff was out of sight, Jay burst into laughter as he bounced on the glass of the store's front window. He slid down against the wall in howling snorts as he pointed up at Duck.

"Did you say, 'Walk of Shane'?" Jay chuckled little machine gun chuckles. Duck started to laugh along with Jay, but slowly, as if he was a little confused.

"You do know it's 'shame', right?" Jay's laugh elevated as he kicked his heels against the pavement in front of the store, and slapped his knuckles against the glass behind him.

"Darrin! He said, 'Shane'!" Jay grasped at Darrin's pant leg, and Duck's face started to turn red as he became embarrassed. "Who in the hell is Shane?"

Darrin wasn't nearly as amused, but he did think seeing Duck get embarrassed was a little funny. He looked in through the glass to see Skylar inside the store, and poked the window to get his attention.

"I just thought it was called that because of some guy named Shane." Duck said, scratching his chin as he tried to make sense of the saying, "Like maybe someone named Shane did it first."

"That's the stupidest thing i've ever heard!" Jay laughed out his last few laughs at the misspoken euphemism, before popping back up to a stance against Darrin to get his attention. "You're still on for tonight, right? Van man?" Jay smirked.

"Yeah, of course, but..." Darrin started, but Jay interrupted with a wave of his arms, sending his right one against the window, tapping it once more.

"Butts, butts, butts...All I see is butts, everywhere I look is butts!" Jay danced as he sang out his custom tune. "Big butts, round butts, baby look at all these butts."

Duck started to grin at Jay's little performance, and soon couldn't help but start to dance along. Darrin was less than thrilled with the interlude.

"But, I want double." He said quickly, ending the little show. "We're using my van. I'm taking more risks. You want me to drive, right? Well, I want double my usual fee."

"I never figured you for the shakedown type." Jay sneered, raising up the corner of his lip, as he looked down at the vet's crutch. "Big military man, gonna move it, huh?" Jay looked over to Duck who didn't seem excited about the extra split, but Duck didn't have a van, and that was really all the motivation Jay needed to make his decision.

"Fine!" Jay shouted out with a grin. "We'll do it for double!"

Jay tapped the glass to signal Teddy to come out of the ice cream store, and Darrin waved at Skylar through the window to hurry him, as well. After a brief moment, Teddy joined in next to Darrin and Jay.

"Yeah, what's up?" Teddy asked the group.

"You and Duck, give me twenty bucks each." Jay demanded, sticking out his hand, impatiently.

The two teens looked at each other, then back at Jay, pulling a twenty dollar bill from each of their pockets and handing it to him. Jay took their bills, and handed them to Darrin.

"There, now you got gas money." Jay insisted. "Call it a down payment. You'll get the rest once we deliver the goods."

"Hey..." Teddy whined, "I was about to get an orange cream and a shit load of jelly beans with that jeffy, son." Jay stared at Teddy until he slumped his shoulders in defeat. Duck held his wallet open, and pouted at its emptiness.

"Yeah, no kidding." Duck added to Teddy's disappointment.

Darrin looked in through the window, again, and Skylar was still wandering around the store, so he tapped the glass again and waved for him to come outside once more.

Skylar turned to see Darrin calling for him, and ran outside. "What, I didn't get anything, yet!" Skylar yelled out.

"We'll get you something at the gas station. Come on." Darrin said, looking down at his little brother. He put his hand on Skylar's shoulder and turned him towards the small parking complex. "I'll see you guys tonight." Darrin pushed Skylar forward to get him moving, and followed behind.

"Yeah, see you tonight..." Jay laughed out. Darrin and Skylar walked down the sidewalk leaving the teen gang behind them. "Double damnit." Jay leaned his back against the glass window, and slapped his palms back.

Suddenly, the ice cream store door burst open again, and the giant muscled lumberjack that worked there popped his head out from the breach.

"Granny said... stop tapping... on the glass." Rando spoke out in his slow growl of a voice. The three boys filled with dread as they gazed into his darkened eye sockets and milky white eyes. His meaty grip pulled at the door knob, slamming the door closed behind him as he re-entered the store.

The three teens ran screaming and laughing down the sidewalk.

14

~ Hellslime ~

When Emily arrived at the RV park, the rest of the police force was already there. She immediately noticed Jacobs' patrol car, torn apart, at the end of the lot. Police tape littered the entire area, and Emily couldn't discern what was and wasn't a crime scene at a glance. Motorhomes and campervans were ripped open like they were made of tin foil, and body parts were all over ground.

Crocker came out from the manager's office to meet the sheriff, and Marlon followed close behind. Their faces were pale, and they had a sick demeanor.

"Holy hell, Emily." Chief Crocker whispered out with a look of shock coating his face. "Don is over there with Jacobs." He said, pointing to the camper at the far end of the yard. "What's left of him."

Emily looked around in disbelief. Closest to her was a pool of the black slime with bits and chunks of bone floating around in it. She bent over to examine it closer, and she could see it still moving around.

"I'll take you over to him." Officer Marlon offered, his voice held an eerie calm, and Emily nodded in agreement.

As they rounded the corner, Emily could see Officer Taylor throwing up behind the manager's building. Another body laid in pieces across the gravel at the entrance to the park, and various pools of ooze puddled in the parking lot.

"We think it's Jacobs." Marlon said as they walked, "There wasn't a body. Just a hand holding Jacobs' sidearm." He explained, preparing Emily for what she was about to see.

"What the...?" Emily stood aghast. Donald Gunther stood next to a large pool of gore and blood as they made their approach. "Holy shit, Roger. I saw the body at the entrance, or what was left of it. How many more are there?"

"All of them, Emily." Roger stated blankly. "The park manager, the tenants, Jacobs...All of them."

"What in the hell does something like this?" Emily asked rhetorically as she looked around the scene leading to Donald. "And don't you dare say a goddamn bear, Roger."

"No way, Sheriff." Marlon said with a serious tone, "Whatever did this is some kind of demon...something evil." There was fear in his voice, and Emily was starting to feel the same way, but she also felt happy that she heard someone else admit there may be something more going on in Bay City.

There was something more going on; something dark, and it would seem that now that darkness was spreading faster. Emily felt it all around her, and she had ever since she entered the little town. Now, she felt more and more like leaving.

Donald knelt down and picked up a stick from the slime pool that was covered in the same black ooze he had been analyzing before. He poked it into the pool of sludge, swirling it in the goo, and as he did it moved along with the stick, pulling what was on the stick off and down, slowly back into the larger pool.

"Anything interesting, Don?" Emily called out from behind the examiner, spooking him, and almost making him fall over into the slime. Emily grabbed him by the back of his collar, and helped him avoid the sticky event, pulling him back and allowing him to right himself to a stance.

"I got you." Emily said as Dondald brushed off his coat and regained his demeanor.

"That could have gotten messy." Donald said with a smile. "Thank you, Sheriff."

Emily looked back at the pool of slime and noticed a severed arm stuck in the sludge, holding a police service sidearm.

"Oh my god! Don, is that the arm?" Emily questioned the doctor in horror.

"That's Jacobs' pistol!" She declared confirming what Roger had told her. "Where's the rest of him?"

"My best guess…" Donald started, as he adjusted his glasses, "Is that is him." He pointed down to the large soupy mass. "Atleast, some of him." The doctor grabbed an evidence bag from his pocket and picked the slimy stick back up, placing it in the bag, and zipping it up tight.

"No shit, Don?" Emily looked to the doctor with a curiously mortified expression.

"No shit, Sheriff." the doctor replied matter-of-factly. "The best I can do is run some tests and see if I can get a DNA match from his file to some of these bits of bone and cartilage to confirm, but honestly…" Donald turned back to look at the arm in the sauce, "…You'll probably get the serial back from the sidearm faster."

Donald put the bag in his examiners case, and stood back up. "Whatever did this was bigger than a bear by a lot."

"How much bigger?" Officer Marlon interjected, "And what do we have around here that's bigger than a bear?"

"I dunno, officer." Donald stared at Roger with wide eyes, making his glasses little panels across his pupils, "Maybe, it isn't from here."

"Aliens again, Don?" Emily rolled her eyes not liking the doctor's professional opinion.

"I'm not saying that, Emily." Donald assured, looking down into the black ooze. "Something more hellish leaves a slime like this..." The doctor's voice rose with his morbid amusement, "That's it! A hellslime!"

Emily disregarded the doctor's absurd evaluation as she eyed the park, "A bear is hard enough to believe, but I know one didn't rip this camper open." She said looking at the large claw marks that tore through the motorhome. "Any word back from the city lab on that goop?" Emily asked.

"Not yet." Donald answered with a hint of dissatisfaction, "They never get to our cases out here very quickly, but I'm sure they're working on it." The doctor sighed, then turned to talk to Officer Marlon directly, "However, I did manage to find your hit and run motor coach, officer. It's right over there." The doctor pointed to Dave and Marta's RV.

"It's still here?" Marlon said in surprise as he turned to see the motorhome still sitting with the television on. "So, did you get an I.D. on the victim?" The officer asked.

"Yes, it came back this morning. We got lucky. His prints were in the database." Donald explained, "James Tucker, A.K.A. Tux, age fifteen. He was a local kid."

He read from a notepad he had stashed away in his breast pocket. "Injuries were consistent with high velocity blunt force trauma to the cranium and upper torso, resulting in death upon impact...presumably with the RV in that lot."

Emily fumed at Roger, "You sure it wasn't a bear attack?"

"I would never falsify my reports, Sheriff," Donald said sternly in Roger's defense, not understanding why Emily was upset. Roger thought back to the night before, about how upset Emily was when she found out about the hit and run murder, but he had hoped her surroundings would make it pale in comparison. "You can go see for yourself. There's still dried blood caked in the wheel well." He insisted.

"Relax, Don. It was a bad joke." Emily quipped. "I think I've seen enough blood this morning. I'll be at the diner, drinking all the coffee." She said, turning to go back to her patrol car. Officer Marlon and Donald Gunther went to check out the suspect motorhome.

Chief Crocker watched as Emily sped away from the scene.

15

~ In that Back Alley ~

The low hanging clouds floated across the afternoon sky, dimming it in the way only the coast knew. The middle of the day looked like dusk, and the town moved just as slow to reflect the weird weather. The salon radio buzzed as Wendy tuned it, searching for a channel with a better signal. Haley sat in the salon chair with an apron around her, in the middle of getting her haircut by Wendy during her lunch break from the diner.

"Damn thing," Wendy slapped the radio with the palm of her hand, "It never wants to work on a cloudy day." She gave up and returned to work on Haley, grabbing up her scissors and starting to trim at the ends of her lengthy hair.

"Did you hear what happened over at the RV park this morning?" Haley asked Wendy ready to return to their gossip session. Her hands flailed around under the draped sheet that protected her from her own clippings as she talked. "I didn't see anything, but I heard that the bear got someone else."

"Oh honey, it was all of them, is what I heard." Wendy tilted her head, running a comb through Haley's hair, and clipping at it seemingly randomly as she talked. "It's all anyone's talking about today; more people getting killed. It's so tragic."

"That's why they got that Sheriff girl out here." Haley suggested, "People keep going missing, or turning up dead. Someone's got to do something about it." Haley watched as Wendy cut, and talked to her through the mirror in front of them.

"I don't know. She could just be here for Roger." Wendy gave a sarcastic smirk, "I saw her coming out of his place this morning." Wendy laughed. "Maybe the county is just making house calls these days."

"No way!" Haley remarked in false shock. "She just stayed at his apartment like that?" She dropped her jaw to show more expression, "Lady get a hotel room." Wendy laughed her rehearsed laugh, and drew back the apron from her client.

"Let's get some toner on there, and rinse. Then, we'll dry you back out." Wendy smiled, and brought Haley over to the sink, and began to massage the product into her hair.

"Yeah, they did a good job sending her. If there is some bear eating everyone, she'd be the last to get eaten. Skinny little bitch." Wendy sneered out humorously, and they both started to laugh.

Wendy finished rinsing out Haley's hair, and then brought her over and her in the large cone-shaped hair dryer. "I'm only going to put you in for a minute or two while I go have a cigarette out back." She explained as she started up the loud machine, and Haley smiled and nodded.

The alley out back was never well lit, even in the daytime. The sunlight sensitive timers on the lights made them flicker all throughout the day, and it gave the alley a creepy aesthetic that Wendy usually enjoyed; however, the dark clouds above crackled with the sounds of a coming storm, and that gave Wendy chills.

She lit her cigarette, and listened as she heard the sounds of people talking at the other end of the alley. It wasn't uncommon for people to hang out there, especially employees of the local shops on the streetside. The back of her salon was tucked in an alcove in the alley, and it let Wendy hide during her smoke breaks.

A drop fell and hit Wendy on the top of the head, causing her to take another puff of her cigarette, and then stomp it out.

"It's raining, already?" She asked out loud in an aggravated scramble to get back inside. She reached up and wiped the liquid from her hand, but when she pulled her hand back down she noticed that it wasn't water on her hand, and that it had stretched down from the top of her hair with her hand, still attached to her head. She panicked as she saw the black slimy substance on her, and started trying to wipe it off on her apron, but it wouldn't detach.

The back door flew open, and the storm crackled outside as the giant creature's oozing tendrils slid down the door frame dripping its tarry flesh onto the ground as it descended into her view. Wendy screamed at the sight of the monster. It opened its mouth revealing its giant sharp gnashing teeth.

She turned and started to run back into the front of the salon, but the hellslime flung its long clawed arm out snatching Wendy around the waist. Once it clamped its grip, Wendy was cut in half.

The hair dryer timer started to beep, and Haley lifted the cone from her head. Now that the machine had turned off and the blowing noise had stopped, she could hear. She looked around for Wendy, but the salon was quiet. An unusual amount of quiet that the salon never was.

"Ms. Pottercorn?" Haley called out to the back. "You still smoking?" She got up to look for Wendy, but stopped as she noticed the clock on the salon wall. "Wendy?" She called out, again.

"I'm going to be late getting back to the diner. I'm just going to leave the money on the counter!" Haley yelled through the little curtain that separated the front and back of the salon. "Wendy?" She called again, now becoming worried that she hasn't gotten a response.

Haley took a step closer to the curtain, and as she did she stepped in something sticky causing her to look down at her shoe. She noticed a pool of black goo forming around her feet, and the curtain drew back revealing the glowing eyes of the large creature filling the doorframe.

It leaned forward, sniffing her with its nose-like cavity. Haley looked up in terror at the slime-dripping, veiny black monster, and it looked deep into her eyes.

Haley was frozen, and unable to scream.

~ Faster for the Pastor ~

"Did you hear that?" Teddy turned and tapped a slack-jawed Duck, leaning against the alley way. Jay stood at the end of the alley on his phone, pacing back and forth.

"I don't hear anything." Duck replied, looking around down the dark corridor.

"I didn't ask if you *'hear'* anything, as in *'current'*. I asked if you *'heard'* anything. Meaning in proximity to the time at which I may or may not have heard something. That being why I asked...confirmation of my own audible sensory perceptions." Teddy lectured in retort, in his usual condescension to Duck. "It was like a real quiet scream." he peered down the dark alley, "You didn't hear it?"

"Man, I can't hear anything over Jay screaming at his phone." Duck shot a sideways glance to their pacing leader. Jay paid no attention to the others while he listened to the voice on the other end of the line. The two went back to peering into the dark alley.

"Darrin is taking his sweet ass time! Feels like he left hours ago." Duck complained.

"It has been hours, you idiot!" Teddy shot back quickly with a sneer of his lip. "He literally left hours ago."

"I told you, we got another driver, everything is going to work out fine." Jay finally speaks out, disgruntled at the person he's on the phone with. "It's a van, everything's gonna fit!" Jay assured and hung up the phone, then turned back to his cohorts.

"Old shits, man." Jay let out in contempt as his friends looked on. Behind him, a shadow began to loom, and Duck and Teddy's eyes grew as a familiar figure emerged around the corner. Jay turned to see a man in his mid-thirties approaching them. He was dimly lit, except for a shimmer that flashed across his eye glasses. Jay knew the man, and his posture immediately stiffened.

"Is everything alright, Jay?" The older man called out as he entered the alley. He carried a briefcase that he sat down on the ground in front of the trio as he stopped. "Am I late?"

"No sir, Father Gary." Jay insisted, a little too anxiously, "I mean. Yes sir, everything is alright, and you're not late at all. We're ready!"

"Yeah, we're ready to go!" Teddy added in agreement with Jay to assure the preacher.

Father Gary was the town's local pastor. It was a relatively new position he had taken at the town's church, replacing the previous preacher after his mysterious disappearance from the town a little more than a year before. Since then Gary Owens had become a staple of the town's social network.

Everyone had come to know Father Gary, for one reason or another.

"Good. Then, everything is in place. You can pick up what you need at eight o'clock when I close the pharmacy." Father Gary assured as he nudged up his glasses with his forefinger, and continued past the boys into the alleyway leaving the briefcase in front of them.

Duck reached down to pick it up, but Jay slapped his hand away, "Hey, that's not for you, hands off." Duck recoiled his hand as Teddy began to laugh. Jay picked up the briefcase, and clicked open the fasteners holding it shut.

All three boys started to spread wide grins across their faces as they looked inside.

"Remember!" Gary called out from down the alley, echoing through the dim corridor, startling Duck, "Eight O'clock!" Then, he disappeared out the other side of the alleyway.

"That guy really gives me the creeps." Duck admitted as he watched over his shoulder to make sure the preacher was gone. Jay snapped the briefcase closed again, and shrugged.

"That's not what he gave me." Jay mused as he patted the tote, and Teddy snorted out another laugh. "Now, Darrin's just got to hurry his ass up and get here, so we're not just hanging. Come on, let's go wait by the pier." Jay waived for the others to follow him as he turned and walked out of the alley holding his prize.

Duck continued to watch behind them as the afternoon started to grow dim, turning their alley into a spooky mass of darkness and twitching sign lights.

"Yeah, let's go wait by the pier" Duck agreed with a gulp as he caught up to his friends.

~ Another Night Out ~

Skylar sat in front of the couch using the coffee table to do his homework as he watched the television. Darrin put away his last dish, and turned off the sink before walking into the living room to give Skylar the bad news.

"Hey, I'm finished with the dishes. How's your homework going?" Darrin eased into a conversation he didn't want to have with his little brother.

"Almost done and ready for Lo'Rana!" Skylar replied in excitement, and it saddened Darrin that he would have to let his brother down by missing their weekly viewing of the popular cartoon; *Lo'Rana and the Dreamraiders*, a new age spin-off of classic cartoons that included cameo appearances of *Mighty Thunder Ray*. It was Skylar's favorite show, and they had watched the new episodes together every week since Darrin had become his guardian.

"Record this one for me." Darrin said as he grabbed his jacket from the kitchen hook, and Skylar spun around to give his older brother a death glare. "I'm sorry!" Darrin said, almost laughing at the little angry face.

"You can always wait, and we can watch it when I get back." Darrin bargained, but he knew that would be asking too much of the youngsters attention span.

Skylar confirmed this by increasing the intensity of his eye beams. Darrin grabbed his crutch from behind the counter, and hobbled into the main room.

"You always do this!" Skylar shouted out as he slammed his book closed. "It's supposed to be our night! This is the episode where we find out how Lo'Rana lost her arm!"

Darrin continued to the door, picking up his keys from the little table beside it.

"I'll make it up to you when I get home. I promise." Darrin said without looking at Skylar as he walked out the door.

Skylar huffed, and swiped his arms across the coffee table, knocking off his books and papers into the floor. After stewing in his anger for a moment, he grabbed the remote control for the television, and turned it off.

The new silence allowed him to hear Darrin's van roar to life, and he crossed his arms and sat back on the couch, still angry. He listened as he heard Darrin pull out of their driveway, and huffed again as he grabbed the remote control, again.

He turned the television back on and sighed out a low growl of disappointment.

"I'm not waiting." he huffed out under his breath.

The television showed a commercial that was coming to an end, and the show's theme song began to play as the intro started. Skylar immediately changed his attitude and became excited, singing along with the song.

He smiled and laughed for a moment, until he instinctively looked over for his absent viewing partner. His smile began to fade again, and Skylar grabbed the remote once more, turning the television back off.

A minute passed as he sat alone in the quiet.

"I'm going to the beach." Skylar told himself, and he got off the couch and left the little house behind to walk the three blocks it would take for him to get to his sandy escape.

16

~ Closing Down the Morgue ~

Donald Gunther found himself strolling through rows of tables lined with bag after bag of evidence in the form of severed limbs and other body parts that he had transported from the scene at the RV park, when he noticed the little red light on his phone system blinking. He had missed a call while he had been in the field. He pressed the button to start playing the message, and the little machine beeped as it began.

"Donald, hi..." The caller started, "This is Jim Watkins over at Metro Labs. I'm calling because I received your sample." Donald's ears perked up as he listened, but he still continued cataloging his mountain of evidence.

"I'm not sure what it is I'm looking at here. The viscosity is off the charts, and the elasticity is like nothing I've ever seen. Where exactly did you find this stuff?" Don picked up a jar that contained some of the black ooze, and stared into it as he listened to his colleague's voicemail. "When you get a chance, give me a call back. We really need to talk about this. In the meantime, I've sent the sample you gave to me to some of my friends at another lab to see if they've ever seen anything like it. Let me know if you find any more."

The message ended, and Donald looked around the lab at dozens of similar samples to the one he was holding. It all seemed to still be alive, moving in their vials, searching to reconnect to each other part. He sat the jar back down on the table and continued over to the body of a teenage boy laying on an exam slab.

"Looks like you're the only one here that died of natural causes." Donald mused as he looked down at the boy's body. He picked up the clipboard that hung from the table, and began to look over his findings when he heard something bubbling at the other end of the exam room. Don turned, but saw nothing other than the glow coming from the row of lamps that hung above his tables and evidence.

"Nothing here is consistent with anything other than Marlon's theory. He was definitely hit by the RV." He said aloud as he read over his own report, and again he had his thoughts interrupted as he heard a gurgling noise coming from behind him. He looked back, but chose to ignore the noise once more as he made his way around the table. As he inspected the corpse he suddenly noticed some of the black slimy substance on the body.

He pulled his phone from his pocket, and dialed Emily's number. The phone rang as Donald paced, waiting for her to answer. The bubbling and gurgling noise became louder as he listened for the other end of the line, but there was no answer, and Emily's phone sent the doctor to her voicemail.

"Emily. It's Don. You need to call me." He said urgently, "There's something up with the black ooze. I just got a call back from Metro Labs and they can't identify it, but I'm definitely starting to think it's the key to this whole thing."

Don suddenly began to feel something drop down onto his head from above. As the black tarry sludge dripped onto his lab coat, he titled his head upward, and saw the drooling open maw of the dark creature stretched above him.

"Oh my god, Emily" Don gasped into the phone as he stared upward at the howling gooey beast, "It's...disgusting." He managed to admit, but only a second before the monster's mouth clamped its jagged rows down onto the doctor, engulfing him from the shoulders up, pinching him in two.

The medical examiner's legs gave out and his torso fell forward to the floor, and Donald joined the rest of the lifeless evidence in the room. His phone slid from his hand as it hit the floor, but continued to record his last message to Emily. It would contain the growls and snorts of the unsatisfied creature.

For a moment, it lingered its snout upwards as if it were getting a scent from something in the air, then, it slithered out of the examiner's lab.

~ A Bad Time for Dick ~

Mayor Adkins was about to walk out the front door of his multi-million dollar beach house mansion when one of the crystal wine glasses he had bought his wife, Glory, shattered against the wall next to his head. Dick's shoulders reared back in surprise as he watched the red wine run down the stark white wall. He turned slowly to see Glory angrily panting in front of him.

"Just exactly where in the hell do you think you're going?" She yelled out, sending a chill down Dick's back, and standing the hairs on his neck upright. "Do you know what time it is?"

Glory was already dressed in her nightgown and slippers, and had been all morning and afternoon. She couldn't stand what her husband was, but maybe it was more that she couldn't stand her husband, but for Dick, it was a mutual feeling.

"Let me guess. It's that hairdresser bitch again, isn't it?" Glory continued to shout as she marched towards the cowardly mayor, her slippers slapping the ground as she came face to face with him.

Dick was still wearing his suit from the work day, and had his leather case in his hand as he prepared to leave. Glory noticed him holding it, and immediately smacked it out of his hands.

When it hit the ground, the strap that held it shut opened, and several large stacks of money fell out onto the floor in front of Glory. When his wife saw the large amount of money, she couldn't control her temper and hysteria. Dick scurried to collect it back into the leather bag.

"Oh my god!" Glory screamed, "You're finally doing it!" She huffed as she began to pace around and around. "You're going to leave me!"

Dick stood with the satchel. "No, goddamn it, I was just going to do some of my own business." He muttered angrily. His eyes were bloodshot red, and his pupils were little dots in the center of rose milk pools as he glared at Glory.

"What business could you possibly be doing at seven o'clock at night with that much money? It's after supper, Dick!" Glory demanded as she bawled her fists at her side. "Goddamnit! Tell me who the hell she is!" She shouted into her husband's face.

This was not the first night or the fiftieth that Mayor Richard Adkins and Glory Adkins fought this fight with one another.

As much as he tried to keep his infidelity from her, Glory still always had a sense that Dick wasn't as faithful as he pretended to be for the citizens of Bay City. She had followed him on several occasions, and had seen him, but he had always denied all of her accusations.

Tonight she would confront him for the last time, she thought.

Dick's shoulders heaved up and down as he became more and more angry. He stood silently staring into Glory's same infuriated eyes.

"Don't just stand there and gawk at me. You're on drugs again, aren't you?" Glory seethed out through her teeth. Dick's nose scrunched as his eyebrows buried themselves at the corners of his eyes.

"I'm the mayor, damnit." He growled out. "I have shit to do, Glory. I don't have time for this!" His voice rose as he spoke, elevating with his anger.

"Oh sure, you're the mayor!" Glory said, rolling her eyes and flailing her arms in the air like she was tossing a pizza. "The mayor of what...a town with hooker hairstylists, junked out teens, and asshole tourists? Good job, Mayor McShithead."

Glory began to pace around again.

"I'm leaving, Glory." Dick reached for the door handle, barely opening the door before his wife pushed him into it, closing the door shut. Out of reflex, Dick swung his hand back, hitting her across the face. Dick stood in shock for a moment, "Oh god...I'm..." Before he could finish his sentence, Glory turned and shoved her slippered foot into Dick's portly stomach, sending him against the door once again.

She then began to pummel him with the bottoms of her fists as he curled over.

"You son of bitch!" She cried out, beating on his back. She pulled away and began kicking at his legs trying to send Dick to the floor. Dick dropped his bag again, and grabbed Glory by her upper arms, holding her at bay. "Let go! Let go! You're hurting me!" She cried out as Dick held her.

"Stop it!" Dick spat out with a lip full of blood. "I'm leaving before one of us gets hurt!" He said as he let her go, and picked up his bag. He turned the door knob, and began to leave Glory behind, and it infuriated her even more. She grabbed one of the terra cotta potted plants that sat on the table next to the door, and slammed it against the side of Dick's skull, shattering the pot and collapsing Dick onto the tile floor in front of the opening door.

The blood began to run across the grooves in the tile as Glory panted, taking deep full chested breaths.

As the door crept open, she could hear the sound of the liquid as it traveled, gooping along, slithering a trail of slime toward the front door. When Glory looked up from her unconscious husband she stared into a black oozing mass.

The tar from its tentacle-like arms dripped down onto the stone stoop.

"Oh my..." Glory screamed as she saw the full form of the creature, and it ignored her as it reached down and picked up the mayor of Bay City in its claw. The monster lifted him from the floor and pulled him out through the doorway and up into the air above. Its eyes flashed as it opened its cavernous jaws, and Dick began to come to. His face held confusion as he began to scream in the creature's grip. Glory screamed with him, but then, the monster snapped its pincer shut.

Dick was cut in half, and Glory's scream hit another pitch. Blood poured out onto the floor in front of her, and she tried to turn but her slippers had very little traction on the tile.

The monster howled as it whipped its other appendage towards Glory.

17

~ As the Sun Dies ~

Rando ran down the pier, chasing after Sheriff Sanders. The boards creaked as he galloped along, making strides to catch up to her. The setting sun made the pier dark and the solar-powered boardwalk lights had all begun to illuminate Emily's path as she felt someone approach behind her.

"Miss!" Rando called out in his guttural low growl, and Emily turned in attack position holding an ice cream cone in her bawled fist, immediately second-guessing the decision upon sight of the large over-sized man. Rando recoiled defensively before sticking out his hand holding a couple of dollar bills and some loose change.

"You forgot...your change..." Rando said nervously slow, but not slow because he was nervous.

"That's fine. You can keep it." Emily relaxed and licked her ice cream, chewing its contents for a second, "You didn't have to run all the way down here to give me back a couple of dollars." She told the blank-eyed giant standing in front of her with a wave. Rando's mouth gaped open as he looked vacantly at her.

"O.k." Rando growled out in his abbreviated way, before crunching the money back in his fist, and turning around to run back down the pier in his same galloping manner. As he did, he passed Officer Marlon heading towards Emily.

"What a weird ice cream man." She muttered to herself as she watched Rando leave. Rando didn't go unnoticed by Roger either, whose pace was hastened as he got closer to Emily until finally meeting her on the pier where Rando left her.

"We need to talk." Officer Marlon told the sheriff intensely.

"Can it wait, Roger? I'm trying to finish this." Emily said, pointing to her cone and taking another big bite out of the top. "How did you know where to find me, anyway?"

Roger smiled. "I know you, Emily." He said, turning to look at the sun setting on the water over the bay, "This was always your favorite spot to go when you got stressed out. That time after basic, when your mom wouldn't let you come home and you had to stay in the inn because you got a tattoo in Clarksville." He laughed a little trying to lighten the mood, "You came here, and when your Aunt Georgia died while you were deployed...when you got back, this was the first place you came. You always come to watch the sun die out."

"When the sun drops just under the horizon, and there's that little flash that goes across..." Emily stared out into the bay with Marlon, "That's the best part." She smiled.

"Well, except for the ice cream. It's tradition. I've been eating Granny's cones since I was a little girl and my parents brought me to this pier. I guess nostalgia helps calm me down." She explained as she pondered the idea herself.

"Well..." Roger turned back to Emily. "I'm going to need you to hold on to that feeling while I tell you something." He said, turning his tone back to a more business-like one.

"What if the thing that's killing everyone isn't a bear?" He asked rhetorically, but that didn't stop Emily's face from turning wry at his question.

"What the hell, Roger? I've been telling you it's not a goddamn bear." Emily's voice rose as her temper became tested.

"Wait...Hear me out." He paused her from becoming more agitated. "What if this hellslime thing knows who it's killing and why...what if it's got a motive?" he asked, and Emily only looked back confused. "What if..." He continued, "It wasn't just at the RV park randomly, but instead it was looking for someone, and everyone else was just collateral."

"I'm not following you, Roger." Emily cocked a brow, "Who would it be looking for?"

"Jacobs." Marlon said almost to himself. "It's all that old man's fault. The damned farmer." Roger thought aloud, ignoring Emily's presence in the conversation as he epiphanized.

"What about farmer Kirkland?" She asked, still confused with what Roger was talking to himself about. Marlon stared off into the sunset, lost in his own thoughts as Emily's mind raced back to the case of Tom Kirkland and the insidious bear mauling. "What does he have to do with Jacob's being murdered?"

"It's a curse." Roger muttered out, still lost in his golden distraction. "It's all because they tried to cover it up." He trailed off in sudden realization.

"What?" Emily asked again, angrily confused. "Cover what up, Roger?" She put her hand on his shoulder and shook him back into the conversation with a hard nudge. "Tell me whatever the hell it is you're trying to tell me. Whole story."

Roger nodded, and gulped as he thought about being hunted by whatever it was that killed all those people at the RV Park. He had lived in Bay City for most of his life, and he knew the town had an eerie ambiance that seemed to permeate throughout it. He had lived within the town's darkness, and wasn't altogether innocent himself.

"It started with the Murphy's son." He said nervously, "The bear mauling last month didn't quite happen the way the case report said." Roger looked deeply remorseful as he searched Emily's aggravated face, looking for her to lessen her elevated guard.

"I knew it!" Emily proclaimed wrathfully, "What the hell was it, Roger?"

"Kirkland." Roger replied with wide eyes, "He shot the kid." He explained as he watched Emily become puzzled once more. "We didn't know when the boy first went missing, but one night at the Fish Hook ole Tom was drunk talking about how he had to chase off some of the teens with a shotgun. If it wasn't for that we'd have never found him out where he was. By the time we did, the kid had been picked on and chewed at. So, Tom and Dick being friends, it got called an animal attack, and Kirkland didn't see any trouble after they found buckshot in the kid's back."

"Holy shit. That's why Sarge left and Crocker took over at the PD." Emily surmised, "But why does that have anything to do with Jacobs?"

"He was the one who found the kid. He's the one who came up with the whole animal attack idea." Roger explained like he had solved an elaborately simple riddle.

"So what? Why does that make Jacobs a target?" Emily probed, still not understanding where Roger's theory was going.

"Becuase! If you saw where we found that kid, you'd understand." Roger implored exasperated, "The only way Jacobs even found that kid was by smell. After Kirkland shot him, the kid had crawled through the mud and pulled himself down into this giant hole in the ground, under a busted and gnarled evil old stump. Probably trying not to get shot again by Tom."

"I'm still not following you, Roger." Emily said impatiently, "It's horrible, but I still don't see how finding the boy puts Jacobs in the crosshairs of some evil bastard hell bent on gruesomely killing people."

"Some evil thing, Emily." Roger stuttered out fearfully. "I was there, too."

"Oh shit, you're still buying that crap." Emily's hands flailed upwards in protest. "This is all starting to make more sense. I knew there was something weird going on here."

Emily started to walk down the pier back to her car, and Roger followed behind her trying to keep up to her pace, "You know how stupid and superstitious you sound?" She questioned over her shoulder at him.

"It's not stupid, Em." Roger said, grabbing her shoulder to slow her. "You tell me. What else could it be?"

Emily spun around to face Roger again, "You want me to believe that some old farmer shot a kid and now there's some demon bear chasing down people and murdering them to avenge his death, or something dumb like that?" Her face twisted with anger, "Stop watching old horror movies, Roger." She turned and huffed, pulling her shoulders down as she marched off.

Emily unlocked her car, and picked up her phone as Roger caught up behind her. As she opened it, the phone displayed a newly missed notification from Donald Gunther.

"Damnit." She huffed again. "I missed the examiner." Emily said back to Roger without looking.

"He's in on it." Roger said bluntly, and Emily ignored him as she played back the missed voice recording, hearing Donald Gunther scream as the creature tore him apart, through the tiny speaker. Marlon's face was mortified by the grotesque noises that came through the line as the monster howled.

"Still think I'm being superstitious?" He said frantically.

"Holy shit!" Emily said, hanging up the phone. "Holy shit, Roger. They killed Don."

"It did, Emily...It." Roger said ominously, and Emily scowled.

"I'm not buying it, Roger, I'm just not. It's not some bear, it's not some demon, and there's no such thing as curses, jinxes, or hocus pocus." Emily growled out. "So, just close the book on it." She insisted. "Who else knows what happened?"

Roger gulped as he counted himself on the list, "Tom and Dick were best friends, so I'm sure he knows. Chief knows. Taylor knows. Shit, half of the force knows, Emily." He explained as Emily sat down in her car, shutting the door behind her, and rolling down the window. "Where are you going?" Roger asked the impatient sheriff.

"I'm going to go have a chat with the mayor, and find out why we're covering up our friend's murders here in Bay City." She explained sternly, "You go back to the station and tell Crocker he's going to need to clean up the examiner's office." Emily started the ignition, "Let Joseph know that i'll be back to talk to him next. Everyone's going to have some explaining to do."

Emily rolled the window back up, and pulled away from the pier, leaving Officer Marlon behind as the rocks spat out from beneath her tires. The sun finally died below the horizon, and Emily sped into the darkness.

18

~ Always the Officer ~

The fog grew thick as Sheriff Sanders drove through the back streets of Bay City. The sun was long gone and the only light that still held in the sky was from the moon. It was becoming dark; the kind of dark that only Bay City knew.

Emily pulled up to a stop at one of the town's three intersections when she saw headlights fastly approaching. As the pair of beams passed her, she recognized Darrin's van speeding down the highway. Emily sighed, flipped on her red and blue lights, and pressed her foot to the floor, quickly catching up to the reckless vehicle zooming down the road.

Darrin pulled the van over to the side of the road, and Emily walked up alongside him with her flashlight drawn. She tapped on his window to have him roll it down, and Darrin complied, revealing himself to Emily with an innocent smile.

"Good evening, Sheriff." Darrin said through the open glass.

"Darrin Bennet. Why are you in such a hurry?" Emily asked in a mildly lecturing tone.

"Oh, sorry about that." Darrin feigned an apology, "This time of night, there's no one out here, and my foot just got a little heavy and my speed got away from me." he shook his metal leg, "I won't let it happen again."

Emily nodded reluctantly, "What are you doing out so late? You leave Skylar at home by himself like that a lot?" She probed as her detective senses kicked in.

"No ma'am. Not a lot." Darrin answered, unfazed by the line of questioning. "Just needed to run to the store."

Emily cocked a brow, "What could you need so bad that you had to speed like that? You were doing fifty-two in a thirty." Emily eyed past Darrin into the van to find just an empty passenger seat with a grocery bag on it. Darrin laughed embarrassingly.

"T.P. sheriff." Darrin gave an odd smile, "We were all out. I found out the hard way." Darrin patted the bag in the seat next to him.

Emilly peered around into the foggy darkness that surrounded her, and then turned back to Darrin, "O.k. yeah that sounds like a pretty shitty situation. Carry on, but keep it to the speed limit the rest of the way." She said as she turned back to her patrol car. Darrin nodded, and gave a salute as he rolled his window back up and started the van, again.

He watched as Emily pulled back onto the street, and drove off in the other direction before he continued onto the blacktop.

"Shit dude, that was smooth!" Jay shot out from the back, "You handled that like a real pro!" He grinned wildly as he crawled up into the front seat.

"Toilet paper!" Duck cried out laughing. "He told her it was toilet paper!"

"How to evade authority was one of the first things I learned in the military." Darrin said with a chuckle as he continued down the highway. The van's headlights pierced through the fog as they made their way.

"It's up here on the right." Jay pointed out to the old *'Adkins Boat Rental'* sign that lingered beside the street.

Darrin pressed the brakes with his replaced foot, and abruptly turned the wheel skidding the van through the curve onto the side road. The crew of teens peeked out through the van windows as they drove through the old boathouse parking lot.

"This is where he wanted to meet us?" Darrin asked as he slowed to snail's pace through the lot. "It doesn't look like anyone is even here." He remarked, looking at the dark windows of the old rental store.

"Yeah man, this doesn't look right." Duck added. "Maybe you should call him and make sure."

Jay looked down at his phone to check the time. They were already running behind after being stopped by the sheriff, and it should have given the mayor plenty of time to beat them there, he thought. Jay became irritated.

"Damn old shits. They never do what they say." He remarked as he dialed Richard Adkins' phone number.

The mayor's phone began to ring in his pocket as Emily stepped over his lower torso. Slime oozed down from the walls around her, and blood pooled the tile floor leading to what little remained of Glory Adkins. Emily pulled her sidearm as the phone's ringer startled her, and she quickly darted her eyes around looking for the sound.

When Emily pulled the phone from Dick's pocket, she accidentally answered the call, but said nothing as she listened to the voice on the other end.

"Hey! Hey, can you hear me?" Jay shouted into the phone. "Hey Dick, you missed the drop. We're here in the van, waiting for you. Where are you?" Emily hung up the phone without saying a word.

"Van?" Emily thought to herself as she inventoried the room's aftermath. "Jesus, just what were you into Dick?" She pulled out her radio and pressed the button to signal dispatch, "This is County Sheriff Emily Sanders, requesting additional units at the mayor's residence on Pine st."

She depressed the button, and awaited a response confirming her request, but nothing came back through the line.

"County unit seven, requesting back-up at the mayor's residence." She spoke into the little machine again, but again nothing came back through.

Emily pulled her phone from her pocket, and dialed Officer Marlon's number. It continued to ring until finally getting through to Marlon's voicemail box, but Emily didn't leave a message, and instead angrily hung up the phone.

"What the hell is going on?" She questioned herself aloud. Emily backed herself to the front door, and holstered her pistol before quickly returning to her squad car.

Jay growled angrily at the dead call he held in his hand. "Did that stupid old shit just hang up on me?" He slammed his fist down on the dash, "Screw this! We'll just have to go back to Gary, and tell him that Dick didn't show!"

"I don't know, man." Duck said with a little fear in his voice, "That guy scares the hell out of me."

"This place scares the hell out of me." Darrin added, "I'm fine with being done for the night." He turned the van to leave the lot, "You really think he's not going to show up with the money?"

"I don't care!" Jay snarled, "I'm done being patsy to the idiots." He crossed his arms, and threw himself back against the seat. "They walk around acting they know what's what, but they never do nothing. When it comes time to do something, these old shits get performance anxiety. Hit it." Jay pointed to the exit, and Darrin gave the van more gas.

"Gary's not going to be happy." Duck reminded Jay, curling into the back seat, where Teddy had been asleep. The noise Duck's jacket made as it rubbed the seat woke Teddy, who had been drooling through his dreams.

"Hey, what?" Teddy asked whoever would hear. Then, came to his senses as he peered around the van to see an angry Jay, and a scared Duck. "Where are we going? We do the thing?" he asked, but Jay and Duck remained silent.

"You can go back to sleep. Nothing's going to happen tonight, Teddy." Darrin assured.

19

~ The Full Extent ~

Officer Marlon drove down the highway back to the precinct when he saw Skylar playing by the beach in the moonlight. Skylar kicked crabs as he waded through the rising tide, and didn't seem to notice the patrol car pull to a stop on the wayside. Marlon got out and walked over to the rocks that led down to the beach and yelled out.

"Hey!" He called, "Hey, kid!" but Skylar couldn't hear him over the crashing waves.

The tide pooled in pockets alongside the artificial jetty where Skylar turned over rocks to find hidden treasures in the shimmering water. It was the perfect time to find sand dollars, and he had lined his pockets with them.

"It's not safe down there!" The patrolman belted out over the roaring tide, waving his arms to try to get the boy's attention. Roger grabbed the rail and started to carefully make his way down the rocky path to the kid, but stopped when he saw something move in the distance from the other side of the beach.

At first, he thought it may have just been light bouncing strangely off a wave, but he suddenly saw it move again behind some of the large rocks that stuck up through the sand.

Roger's eyes grew huge.

He could see it clearly, watching the kid playing in the water. It didn't seem to notice him either, and Roger froze in place.

It was large. It had horns growing from its hulking form, but at the same time didn't seem to have a solid form at all, and its body shifted around like a fluid. Roger could see that its eyes glowed strangely when the moonlight hit them, and had huge appendages that it drug along the beach as it dripped a trail of slime, moving closer to Skylar.

It was a demon and Roger knew it.

"Look out!" Roger involuntarily screamed in a pitch he didn't recognize. Suddenly, the creature turned and saw the officer, and began ignoring the kid who still hadn't heard him. Roger began to back up the rocks as the creature started to make its way along the beach towards the wayside.

Roger turned and began to run, passing his patrol car as he sped towards the police station only a block away, but the creature was fast. Roger could hear it behind him as it made it to the top of the rocky stairwell, and he began running faster until reaching the doors to the station, shutting them behind as he entered.

Officer Marlon began to breathe heavy breaths.

"Chief!" Marlon shouted through the station lobby. He was greeted by Officer Taylor coming out of the clerk's desk. Marlon was frantic as he acknowledged Taylor.

"Hey, Roger we got another one at the salon..." Taylor said, pausing his heightened tone as he read Roger's face, "What's going on, Marlon?" he put his hand on the anxious officer's shoulder, but Roger brushed it off as he searched around the station lobby.

"Hey, didn't you hear me?" Taylor asked his crazed cohort.

"Chief!" Marlon yelled again.

Crocker's office door opened, and then slammed shut again as Interim Chief of Police Joseph Crocker stormed into the lobby.

"What exactly the hell is going on here?" Joseph angrily growled out at the two patrolmen. "You couldn't walk your dumbass another twenty feet? Instead, you're out here yelling through the whole building? You're not bleeding? This better be something, Marlon!"

Roger became nearly hysterical at the sight of the police chief, widening his eyes further as he started to explain, "It knows, chief!" He cried out.

"It what? What knows what? What the hell are you talking about?" Crocker demanded as he glared at the insane man in front of him. "Make some goddamn sense." Then, he looked to Taylor for the same.

"I don't know, chief." Taylor shrugged his shoulders, "He just came in here a second ago, screaming at the top of his lungs like that."

"It knows goddamn it!" Marlon's voice rose, "It knew about Kirkland and Murphy's son. It knew about Jacobs and Donald Gunther. It knows what we did!"

Officer Marlon's hands rose into the air as he exclaimed, and a sharp black tar-covered spike plunged into his back and out through his chest projecting his insides onto the two other men. Then, the spike was retracted, pulling Officer Marlon into pieces that collided with the hard tile floor, and sprayed Roger's blood around the room.

The demon stood at the door of the precinct, dripping its slime, and looking at the two policemen with its glowing eyes.

Both men immediately pulled their sidearms and started to fire as they backed into the hallway behind them. The bullets pelted the monstrous figure but only lodged into its gelatinous body, and splattered bits of it against the walls around the lobby.

"Holy shit, Chief!" Taylor cried out, "It's bulletproof!"

The monster twisted and its tendril-like arm whipped through the air as it howled. Its claw clamped down onto Officer Taylor at the shoulders, and peeled away his head as it returned to the creature. Taylor's body went limp as it fell to the floor in front of the police chief, blood draining out from the wound.

Crocker turned and ran down the corridor to escape, but when he reached the exit doors, they were locked. His keys were still sitting on his office desk. Crocker pulled and pulled at the door handle, but it wouldn't budge. The creature crept through the hall behind him.

Joseph turned and the creature grew closer. He fumbled to reload his revolver with the speedloader, but finally managed to snap in the rounds. He pulled up the gun to aim, and the creature flung its oozing arm at the police chief.

Crocker ducked, and the razor-sharp claw slammed into the emergency exit, punching through the steel door.

His eyes widened, and he took aim. Crocker pulled the trigger as many times as the five round cylinder would allow until the shots ended with a click, and then he pulled again to make sure, but the creature stood undamaged.

"Dear god!" Joseph Crocker gasped, "Just die you bastard!" He screamed, and the creature pulled its arm from the door, but it didn't retract. Instead it fell to the floor, and the monster twisted its body, snatching Crocker around the neck like a whip with its arm..

The creature hoisted the police chief into the air and pulled him close to its stretching mouth. Crocker squirmed as he gripped the tentacle that wrapped around him, choking and searching for air. Its eyes widened and the glow began to engulf Crocker.

"No god..." The demon spoke in a hollow voice that echoed through the space between them. "Not... for you." It rasped out slowly as it began to tighten its grip on the man it held. Crocker kicked his legs as the blood left his head. The bones in his neck crunched as the monster squeezed, and blood ruptured from around his nose and eyes.

The creature sniffed at the man, and opened its mouth further as it swallowed the police chief.

20

~ The Lord's Work ~

The old van sputtered as it pulled through town and into the condo parking garage on main street, later than expected. Darrin parked the old beater in one of the spaces next to a black sedan with tinted windows, and as he cut the engine off, Gary the preacher got out of the car next to them. He was still wearing his sunglasses, even though the sun had long since set and a black suit that didn't match the day.

Jay jumped out from the passenger side and walked around to meet Gary at the rear of the van. "We got stood up!" Jay moaned out, shrugging to Gary. He held his phone up for the preacher to see, and it showed several attempted calls. "We waited for him and everything, but he's not even answering his phone."

Duck and Teddy got out from the back of the van, and Darrin stayed seated in the driver's chair with the window down. Gary flicked his thumb across his teeth in thought as he leaned against the back of his sedan.

"I can't believe we got scammed!" Duck sighed, collapsing his arms to his hips, and Teddy began pacing frantically.

"You don't think the cops are going to show up here do you?" Teddy asked as he chewed on his thumbnail. "The guy was the goddamn mayor. He's friends with all the pigs." The teen continued to worry. Duck's head perked towards Teddy, and he cocked a brow.

"No way, man. That guy was as crooked as a dog's hind leg, and addicted." Jay noted passively to try to calm the other two teens. Darrin stayed relaxed as he opened the door, stepped out of the van on his good leg, and joined in the circle. Teddy continued to pace around, making exaggerated motions with his arms.

Gary stayed silent as he watched them, and Jay watched Gary with a worried look on his face.

"Look, there's not much we can do if the guy doesn't show up, am I right?" Jay suggested with a slight shrug of his shoulders and a grin, but his face soured when Gary had no response. The teens reflected back in the preacher's lenses, and Gary remained silent as he stared at them.

In the distance, they began to hear the sound of police sirens as Emily sped back to the police station.

Duck began to panic along with Teddy, and both boys paced in the garage.

"Oh shit." Duck winced as dread began to take hold of his body. "Teddy was right!" he began to whimper in expectation of their arrest. "They're coming this way!" Duck danced around in erratic steps as he lost control of himself.

Gary popped forward from his trunk and slapped Duck across the mouth with the back of his hand, knocking him to the pavement of the parking garage.

Teddy and Jay immediately stepped towards Gary, but the preacher put his hand inside his jacket and pulled out a forty-five long barrel revolver, prodding it into Jay's chest.

"You stupid kids!" Gary snarled out. His eyebrows crushed into the rims of his glasses as he shoved Jay with the pistol. "You thought you could screw up, and just show up here empty-handed?" Gary moved the pistol to Teddy, who curled in fear, then to Darrin who had no reaction. Then, the preacher turned the gun back on Jay.

The boys began to back away as Gary's shadow began to grow. "You dumb little shits were supposed to bring me my money!"

"Hey, just take it easy." Darrin urged Gary, but the large man's shadow again grew larger. Duck got up from the ground holding his lip and joined the other teens, holding up his hands in surrender to the preacher. Gary pinned Jay against the side of the van at gunpoint.

"If you say you're going to do something, you do something!" Gary's hand shook, and the barrel of the pistol wobbled around in the air in front of him.

"Don't shoot him!" Teddy cried out, trying to distract Gary. When he did, Gary's shadow grew twice as big, and suddenly opened its glowing eyes. The thing behind Gary wasn't a shadow at all, but instead a completely different type of darkness.

Gary began to squeeze the trigger on the gun he held at Jay, but in that same moment, Darrin pushed Jay out of the line of fire as the creature behind Gary spun its claw up through the preacher's torso, severing his gun arm from the rest of his body. Blood erupted into the air, and the creature howled as Gary's arm slid across the garage floor towards Duck.

Jay ran towards the driver's door of the van, looking back at Darrin with his hands out, "Keys!" He yelled to Darrin around the giant horned slime creature. He threw Jay the keys and scurried around to the other side of the van as Duck looked down at the arm holding the gun.

Teddy jumped inside of the van's sliding door, and Jay started up the old machine. Before Darrin could get to the passenger door, he felt something pull at the strap that held on his prosthetic leg, then he was tugged back around to the other side of the van and lifted off the ground by the black tarry monster.

Duck grabbed the severed arm, and pried the revolver loose from the dead man's grip. He aimed up at the black demon, and pulled the trigger. The kick from the weapon sent him stumbling backwards, but he managed to hit the creature in the arm that held Darrin, forcing the monster to flail. When it did, Darrin's leg detached and he was thrown through the air across the parking garage.

The hellslime turned its attention towards Duck with a roar that echoed through the concrete walls of the garage. Duck fired the revolver again, but this time hit the monster in the chest and got no reaction as it continued to advance.

Jay put the van in gear, and stepped on the accelerator, reversing into the creature, and crushing it against one of the garage's columns. Duck jumped into the passenger's seat and slammed the door. Jay quickly switched gears and pressed the gas again, but the van didn't move.

"Come on, go! Go! Go!" Duck yelled, and Teddy gripped the back of the front seats. As the van started to grind forward, the teens could hear the sound of metal starting to whine as it tore apart. The back door of the van flew off, and revealed the open mouth of the creature.

The ripping sound continued as Jay desperately stomped on the gas pedal. Duck still held the pistol and pointed it back towards the open door.

"Move!" Duck shouted as he fired another shot past Teddy into the creature, but he still didn't have any effect on the monster. The sound clanged loudly inside the van forcing the boys to cover their ears, disoriented.

The van began to shake as the tarry arms of the hellslime ripped at its rear, jostling the boys around inside. Its tires squealed as they rubbed the concrete, but only spun in place. Duck dropped the pistol on the floorboard of the back seat.

Teddy reached down to grab the forty-five, but as he did, the slimy claw of the creature wrapped around his body and pulled him back over the seat.

"Teddy!" Duck yelled out, throwing his hand out to try to catch his friend, but it was too late. The monster had pulled Teddy out from the back of the Van, digging into him with his long fanged teeth.

Jay pressed the gas harder, and the metal tearing sound came to a climax as the back axle ripped free from the van's undercarriage, sling-shotting the vehicle away from the monster on its front wheels, and out of the parking garage.

Blue and red lights from Emily's patrol car illuminated the street as she approached. The police station was only a block from the parking garage, and before the sheriff could pull in, she stomped on her brakes as the van went by.

Before she could blink, it crashed into a fire hydrant in front of the ice cream shop on the other side of the street. Emily opened the door to her patrol car, and drew her sidearm.

"Darrin!" Skylar's voice shouted from the sidewalk behind Emily. He had seen everything she had while he was walking home from the beach. Skylar began to run towards the van when water suddenly burst from the hydrant, and went gushing into the air without stopping.

"Skylar!" Emily called out as she started to run over to the boy, "Wait!"

Skylar staggered as his knees buckled upon sight of the creature. Its long arms grabbed the remainder of the van, and drug it across the asphalt. The van doors opened and Jay and Duck jumped from the vehicle, both running in different directions.

Duck hobbled as he ran, and the creature quickly snatched him by the shoulder with its long slimy claw. It pulled Duck towards its mouth, and Duck screamed. Jay looked back to see blood erupt from the monster's maw as it devoured Duck.

Jay ran to the door of Granny's Ice Cream and Treats, but it was locked. He tugged and tugged at the handle as the water from the hydrant poured down around him, panicking as he watched over his shoulder. Then, the creature turned towards him.

Skylar turned and began to run back to Emily, who stood in the middle of the road with her weapon drawn. She fired off a round, but it didn't deter the hellslime from going after Jay. Its arm flung forward, and grabbed the teen around the waist.

"Help!" Jay yelled as he pulled one last time at the door, and then he was ripped away by the demon.

It only took a moment before the monster was done with Jay, and had set its sights on Skylar. Emily fired another round to try to slow the creature down, but it only seemed to advance faster as Skylar began to run harder. Emily fired again, and again as she walked toward the black oozing form.

"Keep running, Skylar!" Emily shouted as she fired.

Finally, the creature changed its focus, and stopped, watching the sheriff as she reloaded her pistol. She did quickly, and fired off another round into the creature doing little to harm it. Skylar ran down the street past Emily, and she continued firing round after round.

"That's right, you ugly bastard. You come after me, now." Emily growled out as she fired a round that hit the monster in its glowing eye.

The creature howled into the air, and whipped its body as it flung its long pincer arm toward Emily, severing her arm and tossing her back onto the street. Emily screamed as she tried to pull the trigger on her gun, and realized her arm was missing from the elbow down.

Shock started to set in as she saw the small pool of blood beside her already sealed severed arm. Then, the monster crawled over the top of her.

"Your fear..." It rasped slowly down at the sheriff, "it smells...delicious."

"Emily!" Skylar yelled as he watched the monster hover over her, and the sheriff tried to crawl toward her severed hand, still holding her weapon. The monster wrapped its long clawed arm around Emily's neck, and started to squeeze.

Emily started to lose consciousness.

Then, the bell on the ice cream store's door rang out.

21

~ Keeping the Dark at Bay ~

"Ha...Ha." Rando imitated his hero's signature catchphrase in his own metered tone as his fist slammed into the side of the creature. The impact made the slime-covered monster recoil and loosen its grip on Emily, retracting its oozing tendril as it teetered off-balance. Emily gasped for air as she regained awareness, and Rando stood over her facing the creature down, still wearing his white work apron.

Skylar watched from behind the sheriff's patrol car as Emily drug herself away from the creature while it turned back towards Rando.

"Hmm..." Rando grumbled as the black tarry monster stood at its full height, heaving in front of him, dwarfing him in size. "It only takes one...in the cartoon." He looked down at his fist, a weapon he had never used before, covered in black ooze.

"Gross." Rando murmured out, flicking his fingers clean.

The demon howled at the large and brawny man, and whipped its claw towards Rando. It clamped down around his forearm as he guarded the attack, and the monster began to squeeze. Rando grabbed the pincer with his free hand and pulled, tearing it free from his arm, holding it out in front of him as he inspected it.

Blood ran down Rando's arm from where the claw had gripped him, and Rando looked down to check his wound.

"Ouch!" He growled out loudly, and shook his arm. The blood dripped off onto his work clothes, and Rando huffed in disappointment. He let go of the creature's claw and it retracted it. Rando then took off his stained apron.

Emily crawled until she was at a safe enough distance that she could try to stand, and hobbled back to the cruiser holding her severed arm at the nub.

"Are you ok?" She asked Skylar, panicked. He nodded in return as he continued to watch over Emily's shoulder. The monster howled again as the water beat down around it and the large man that stood in opposition to it. Steam rose from the beast as the drops pelted against its slimy body.

Emily's arm, despite being cut off, had been cauterized by the creature's blade. She reached into her patrol car, and opened the glove box to retrieve her backup sidearm.

Skylar drew closer as he watched the two dark figures face off.

Rando and the creature circled around each other, neither advancing towards the other, but instead each seemed to be testing the other's will. Then suddenly, the demon sprang forward, lunging at Rando and landing on top of him. Ooze dripped from the creature's mouth as it pushed its teeth toward the ice cream scooping lumberjack.

"Get off!" Rando grunted as he heaved the monster up off of his body. As he lifted the creature, Rando stood back up, and threw the sludge beast across the pavement. Slime coated the asphalt as it skidded over to the shoulder of the road.

"Whoa!" Skylar shouted out in excitement, and Rando turned to see the boy.

As they met eyes, Skylar saw Rando's blank white pupils shining in the moonlight, hidden in the dark sockets that surrounded them. Rando nodded to Skylar, but only a moment before the monster's long clawed tentacle arm snatched Rando from his spot and yanked him across the street to the creature.

It held the sleeveless and muscular Rando in the air, and he squirmed to free himself from the monster's grasp.

"What...are...you?" The black void snarled into Rando's face, flinging its tar and slime as it spoke. Rando winced as the snot pelted against him.

"Me?" Rando gruffed out, eyeing the thing's gnarled tines and tarry body, "What...Ugly...Gross thing...are you?" Rando pushed his muscles against the creature's grip trying to free himself, but the monster was strong.

"I am...Darkness!" The hellslime answered in its slithering speech. "I am...hungry." It sniffed at Rando as it held him closer. "You smell...familiar." It snapped its teeth, making a loud clanging sound that Rando could feel in his body. Then, it began sniffing again.

"Yes..." It seethed out, "You also lived...in Darkness." The creature's teeth dripped with black sludge, and Rando pulled away as much as he could to avoid the smell of the monster's breath. "You were so...Afraid. So...Alone." It seemed to grin as it mocked him, "For so...long."

"I live with Granny...now." Rando grimaced as he struggled against the monster. "I give ice cream...to kids!" He growled out as he opened his jaw wide and bit down on the creature's groping arm, sinking his teeth into the black goo.

A shot rang out as Emily fired her revolver into the demon's side, and then another as the sheriff hobbled toward the creature shooting. The beast reared up and turned to face her, still holding Rando, wiggling him in the air.

Ooze dripped from the holes the impacts had made, and Rando kicked the monster in one of its horned mandibles. The creature howled, releasing the hefty bearded Rando back to the pavement with a thud.

It turned and chased towards the one-armed gun-toting sheriff. It was fast, and it leaped forward to make up space between it and Emily, when suddenly the oozing mass was pulled down from the air and into the gravelly asphalt. It roared in anger, and turned back to see Rando pulling at one of its tentacles.

Rando gripped the slippery skin of the monster, crushing down into its flesh, and it flung its bladed arm back trying to get free. Rando pulled away as its claw passed across his chest, cutting his plaid undershirt. Rando's muscled arms flexed as he lifted the huge creature and twisted, throwing it back towards the ice cream shop and away from the kid and the sheriff.

The water still rained down from the open main, and when it hit the creature's skin it began to steam again. This time, there was a lot of steam, and it filled the street billowing towards Rando and Emily. The hellslime became a silhouette in the mist it had made, and Rando searched around with his blank eyes to find the beast.

Emily slumped towards the ground, and Skylar ran to her side.

"Miss Emily!" Skylar cried out, and Rando turned his attention to the boy as the fog surrounded them. In the distance, they could hear the creature howl as it moved around, shrouded by the dense steam. Rando searched around frantically trying to guard against the evil being.

"Yes...Be afraid!" It belted out loudly through the cloud that the three huddled in. Then, the fog separated around the creature's clawed appendage as it flew through the thick air, slapping against Rando's shoulder, and cutting into him.

"Ouch!" Rando winced out, clasping at his wound, and the retracting claw flew back past him as it returned to the monster.

"Look out!" Skylar yelled out to warn Rando as a giant shadow descended down upon them. Rando looked up to see the fog dispersing around the emerging hellslime as it dove onto him from above. It slammed the large man to the ground, and they began to roll away, swirling off into the mist. Skylar could hear Rando grunt as thunderous popping noises came through the cloud.

Rando pounded his fist into the monster as they fought through the fog, and the creature howled, flailing its arms. It ripped at Rando's already torn shirt, and Rando gripped its pincer with one claw in each of his hands, pulling it open wide; wider than it was meant to go, and suddenly a tendon shredding sound came snapping out of the creature's deadly hand.

The beast screamed as it whipped its other arm around to lasso Rando, and pulled him away.

Rando stood facing the creature, watching as the water steamed off its skin. Then, Rando looked past the monster to the fire hydrant, still gushing. The monster snarled and snapped its teeth at Rando, but Rando remained calm and thought about the water, and how it burned off as it hit the monster.

The creature twisted fast, and hurled its whipping tentacle towards Rando, but Rando started to charge towards the hellslime, ducking under it as it passed. He leaned forward and rammed the monster with his shoulder, taking it to the ground. The creature's mouth stretched open as it howled, and it tried to chomp down onto Rando with its large teeth as he leaned back to bring up his fist.

It snapped its teeth, but missed Rando, clamping its mouth shut hard.

The burly large man brought his fist down into the creature's chomping grin, smacking his knuckles against the rock-hard surface. Rando pulled back his bloody fist, and tried again with his other hand. Again, his knuckles slammed against the creature's teeth, and again Rando pulled back a blood dripping fist.

The creature knocked Rando off with a flip of its tentacle, tossing him to the pavement. Then, it jumped up and charged at Rando, and leaped on his back. The creature reared its head back, and then took a forceful bite that would have taken off Rando's arm up to the shoulder, but at the moment the monster bit Rando, he tensed up, and the demon's teeth shattered against Rando's skin like rock candy.

The monster hissed as it pulled away, but Rando grabbed it by the arm again and pulled the thing closer, ramming his bruised fist into the side of the creature's face. Without hesitation, Rando grabbed it by the back and slammed it against the pavement.

The creature's appendages flailed wildly.

Rando began to drag the monster toward the fire hydrant. It whipped its tentacles weakly, beating against him to try to free itself, but Rando endured the clubbing as he pulled the creature across the asphalt. The more water that hit the creature, the more it steamed around them, and Rando tugged its arm across the geyser. He held it there as the pressure pushed the water against the creature's whipping snapper.

After only a moment, the monster's arm started to harden, losing its gelatinous texture. Rando's eyes widened at the discovery, and he felt how brittle the monster's arm was in his hands. Rando twisted his grip, and snapped the monster's arm from its body. The hellslime screamed in pain. Rando tossed it to the ground, and when it hit the pavement, the monster's clawed arm turned to a powdery sand, bursting apart upon impact.

The monster dashed away from the water and Rando to nurse its wounds, but Rando dashed after it. Before the monster could respond, he had it gripped by one the horns protruding from its head and slammed it against the ground again, and then again. Rando growled as he pummeled the monster into the asphalt.

"I missed...so many...episodes!" Rando huffed out as he smashed. The monster squished against the ground, and tar and slime splattered all around them. "I never had...ice cream!" Rando cried out painfully.

The creatures remaining arms whipped, becoming more lifeless with every impact, and Rando didn't stop. He couldn't. Rando thought back through the long years of darkness. He remembered all the nights he stared out through the hole, dreaming of a different life.

Rando, with tears streaming down his face, snatched the monster up from the ground and heaved it up onto his shoulders. He began to walk back over to the water, to the thing he knew would end the creature, once and for all.

"I'll never...let you hurt...anyone....ever again!" Rando shouted as he brought the steaming creature down off his shoulders and through the water, impaling it on what remained of the metal hydrant. The monster howled, and whipped its appendages violently, but as the water filled the monster, its skin began to harden like it had before, becoming brittle.

Rando heaved as he watched the monster lose its purplish-black color, and turn to a lighter dark gray stone. It took a few minutes, but the creature eventually stopped moving and petrified where it stuck.

Rando sighed, and relaxed his shoulders. The monster was dead.

A noise hit the pavement behind Rando, spooking him back into a defensive stance, but only for a moment as a small rock Emily had accidentally kicked rolled by. She hobbled towards him with her arm draped over Skylar's shoulder.

Rando relaxed again as he looked at them.

"Are you...O.k?" Rando asked naively as he watched the bloodied sheriff approac. Emily squinted in pain, looking down at the solidified slime monster, and could help but shake her head.

"I don't think any of us are going to be O.k." Emily replied as she stood, looking down at her arm. "I don't think we'll ever be O.k. ever again."

"O.k." Rando confirmed.

...You gotta find that light.

Epilogue

~ No Sympathy from the Devil ~

"I've been telling ya, Louie, they're something special." The bearded old man spoke out in his golden voice as he moved his pawn forward on the chess board. He was dressed in an all white leisure suit with a long matching colored beard and eyebrows that grew in the same wild fashion.

"Check, by the way." He chuckled as though he had only just realized the severity of his move, as it had cleared the way for another piece.

"You won't always win." His opponent slithered out, "I couldn't break your champion psychologically, nor beat him physically..." Lou scratched his chin as he stared down at the sparse game board.

"Champion?" The white old man laughed again, interrupting his slightly younger-looking rival's thoughts. "You think that was my best move? How long have we been playing this game for now, Lou?"

Lou's angry hand slammed down on the table, shaking the pieces.

"You won't always win!" Lou growled out at his older counterpart. "You haven't won this time! I still have plenty to play with." He assured as he reached to make his next move.

Lou sat dressed in a gray pin-striped suit with black and red accents as the morning sun shined down upon the two of them at the park table. His hand nervously grabbed for one piece, but then another, until a grin came across his face and he picked up his knight.

"I still have champions of my own." He sneered out with a rasp.

...to be Continued.

Stay Tuned!

Frankie will Return in

E.S.Z.S
EVIL SUCCUBUS ZOMBIE SLAYER

Coming Soon!

www.ingramcontent.com/pod-product-compliance
Lightning Source LLC
Chambersburg PA
CBHW071908220626
47052CB00002B/255